SELECTED WORKS BY JAMES SALLIS

Novels Published by No Exit Press

The Long-Legged Fly – Lew Griffin Book One, 1992
Moth – Lew Griffin Book Two, 1993
Black Hornet – Lew Griffin Book Three, 1994
Death Will Have Your Eyes, 1997
Eye of the Cricket – Lew Griffin Book Four, 1997
Bluebottle – Lew Griffin Book Five, 1998
Ghost of a Flea – Lew Griffin Book Six, 2001
Cypress Grove – Turner Trilogy Book One, 2003
Drive, 2005
Cripple Creek – Turner Trilogy Book Two, 2006
Salt River – Turner Trilogy Book Three, 2007
The Killer Is Dying, 2011
Driven, 2012

Other Novels

Renderings
What You Have Left: The Turner Trilogy

Stories

A Few Last Words
Limits of the Sensible World
Time's Hammers: Collected Stories
A City Equal to my Desire

Poems

Sorrow's Kitchen
My Tongue In Other Cheeks: Selected Translations

As Editor

Ash of Stars: On the Writing of Samuel R. Delany
Jazz Guitars
The Guitar In Jazz

Other

The Guitar Players
Difficult Lives
Saint Glinglin by Raymond Queneau (translator)
Chester Himes: A Life
A James Sallis Reader

CRIPPLE CREEK

Turner Trilogy Book Two

JAMES SALLIS

This edition published in 2012
by No Exit Press, an imprint of
Oldcastle Books Ltd.,
P.O.Box 394,
Harpenden,
Herts, AL5 1XJ

www.noexit.co.uk

ISBNs
978-1-84243-732-2 PB
978-1-84243-733-9 kindle
978-1-84243-734-6 epub
978-1-84243-735-3 pdf

2 4 6 8 10 9 7 5 3 1

Typeset by Avocet Typeset, Chilton, Aylesbury, Bucks
Printed and bound by CPI Group (UK) Ltd, Croydon, CR0 4YY

**For further information about Crime Fiction
visit crimetime.co.uk / @crimetimeuk**

To my brother John
and beloved sister Jerry –
in memory of our search for food
somewhere near where Turner lives

The blood was a-running
And I was running too…

—*Charlie Poole
and the North Carolina Ramblers*

Chapter One

I'd been up to Marvell to deliver a prisoner, nothing special, just a guy I stopped for reckless driving who, when I ran his license, came back with a stack of out-standings up that way, and what with having both a taste for solitude and a preference for driving at night and nothing much on the cooker back home, I'd delayed my return. Now I was starved. All the way down County Road 51 I'd been thinking about the salt pork my mom used to fry up for dinner, squirrel with brown gravy, catfish rolled in cornmeal. As I pulled onto Cherry Street for the drag past Jay's Diner, the drugstore and Manny's Dollar $tore, A&P, Baptist church and Gulf station, I was remembering an old blues. Guy's singing about how hungry he is, how he can't think of anything but food: *I heard the voice of a pork chop say, Come unto me and rest.*

That pork chop, or its avatar, was whispering in my ear as I nosed into a parking space outside city hall. Don Lee's pickup and the jeep were there. Our half of the building was lit. Save for forty-watts left on in stores for insurance purposes, these were the only lights on Main Street. I hadn't, in fact, expected to find the office open. Lot of nights, if one of us is gone or we've both worked some event, we leave it unattended. Calls get kicked over to home phones.

Inside, Don Lee sat at the desk in his usual pool of light.

"Anything going on?" I asked.

"Been quiet. Had to break up a beer party with some of the high school kids around eleven."

"Where'd they get the beer—Jimmy Ray?"

"Where else?"

Jimmy Ray was a retarded man who lived in a garage out back of old Miss Shaugnessy's. Kids knew he'd buy beer for them if they gave him a dollar or two. We'd asked local stores not to sell to him. Sometimes that worked, sometimes it didn't.

"You got my message?"

"Yeah, June passed it on. Good trip?"

"Not bad. Didn't expect to find you here."

"Wouldn't be, but we have a guest." Meaning one of our two holding cells was occupied. This seldom enough to merit surprise.

"It's nothing, really. Around midnight, after I broke up the kids' party, I did a quick swing through town and was heading for home when this red Mustang came barreling past me. Eighty-plus, I figure. So I pull a U. He's got the dome light on and he's in there driving with one hand, holding a map in the other, eyes going back and forth from road to map.

"I pull in close and hit the cherry, but it's like he doesn't even see it. By this time he's halfway through town. So I sound the siren—you have any idea when I last used the siren? Surprised I could even find it. Clear its throat more than once but it's just like with the cherry, he's not even taking notice. That's when I go full tilt: cherry, siren, the whole nine yards.

"'There a problem, Officer?' he says. I'm probably imagining this, but his growl sounds a lot like the idling Mustang. I ask him to shut his engine off and he does. Hands over license and registration when I ask. 'Yeah, guess I did blow the limit. Somewhere I have to be—you know?'

"I call it in and State doesn't have anything on him. I figure I'll just write a ticket, why take it any further, I mean it's going to be chump change for someone in his collector's Mustang, dressed the way he is—right? But when I pass the ticket to him he starts to open the door. 'Please get back in your car, sir,' I tell him. But he doesn't. And now a stream of invective starts up.

"'There's no reason for this to go south, sir,' I tell him. 'Just get back in your car, please. It's only a traffic ticket.'

"He takes a step or two towards me. His eyes have the look of someone who's been awake far longer than nature ever intended. Drugs? I don't know. Alcohol, definitely—I can smell that. There's a friendly bottle of Jack Daniels on the floor.

"He takes another step towards me, all the time telling me I don't know who I'm messing with, and his hands are balled into fists. I tap him behind the knee with my baton. When he goes down, I cuff him."

"And you tell me it's been quiet."

"Nothing we haven't seen a hundred times before."

"True enough… He get fed?"

Don Lee nodded. "Diner was closed, of course, the grill shut down. Gillie was still there cleaning up. He made some sandwiches, brought them over."

"And your guy got his phone call?"

"He did."

"Don't guess you'd have anything to eat, would you?"

"Matter of fact, I do. A sandwich Patty Ann packed up for me, what? ten, twelve hours ago? Yours if you want it. Patty Ann does the best meatloaf ever." Patty Ann being the new wife. Lisa, whom he'd married months before I came on the scene, was long gone. Lonnie always said Don Lee at a glance could pick out the one kid in a hundred that threw the cherry bomb in the toilet out at Hudson Field but he couldn't pick a good woman to save his life. Looked like maybe now he had, though.

Don Lee pulled the sandwich out of our half-size refrigerator and handed it to me, then put on fresh coffee. The sandwich was wrapped in wax paper, slice of sweet pickle nestled between the halves.

"How's work going on Val's house?" he asked.

"She's got three rooms done now. Give that woman a plane, a chisel and a hammer, she can restore anything. Yesterday we started sanding down the floor in one of the back rooms. Got through four or five coats of paint only to find linoleum under that. 'There's a floor here somewhere!' Val shouts, and starts peeling it away. Sometimes it's like we're on an archaeological dig, you know? Great sandwich."

"Always."

"Eldon Brown's come by some days to pitch in, says it relaxes him. Always brings his old Gibson. Thing's beat to hell. He and Val'll take breaks, sit on the porch playing fiddle tunes and old-time mountain songs."

Don Lee poured coffee for us both.

"Speaking of which," I said, "I was sitting out front noticing how *this* place could use a new coat of paint."

Don Lee shook his head in mock pity. "Late-night wisdom."

Early-morning, actually, but he had a point. Beat listening to what the pork chop had to tell me, anyway.

"We're way past due on servicing the Chariot, too."

The Chariot was the jeep, which we both used but still thought of as belonging to Lonnie Bates. Lonnie'd been shot a while back, went on medical leave. When the city council came to ask me to take his place I told them they had the wrong man. *You fools have the wrong man,* was what I said. Graciously enough, they chose to overlook my ready wit and went ahead and appointed Don Lee as acting sheriff. He was a natural—just as I said. I'd never seen a man more cut out for law enforcement. I would agree to serve temporarily, I told city council members, as his deputy. Snag came when Lonnie found he liked his freedom, liked being home with his family, going fishing in the middle of the day if he had a mind to, taking hour-long naps, watching court shows and reruns of *Andy Griffith* or *Bonanza* on TV. Now we were a year into the arrangement and *temporarily* had taken on new meaning.

Headlights lashed the front windows.

"That'll be Sonny. He was at his mom's for her birthday earlier. Couldn't break loose to tow in the Mustang till now."

We went out to thank Sonny and sign the invoice. Probably he was going to wait a couple or three months for payment. We knew that. He did too. The city council and Mayor Sims forever dragged feet when it came to cutting checks. Just so she'd be able to meet whatever bills had to be paid to keep the city viable, payroll, electric and so on, the city clerk squirreled away money in secret accounts. No one talked about that either, though it was common knowledge.

"Could be a while before you get your fee," I told him as I passed the clipboard back.

"No problem," Sonny said. In the year I'd known him I'd never heard him say much of anything else. I just filled up, out front. No problem. Jeep's pulling to the right, think you can look at it? No problem.

Sonny's taillights faded as he headed back to the Gulf station to trade the tow truck for his Honda. Don Lee and I stood by the Mustang. Outside lights turned its red a sickly purple.

"You looked it over at the scene, right?" I said.

"Not really. Kind of had my hands full with junior in there. Not like he or the car was going anywhere."

Don Lee pulled keys out of the pocket of his polyester-cum-khaki shirt.

Inside, whole thing smelling of patchouli aftershave and sweat, there was the half-bottle of Jack Daniel's, the crumpled map like a poorly erected tent on the passenger seat, an Elmore Leonard paperback with the cover ripped off on the floor, some spare shirts and slacks and a houndstooth sport coat hanging off the back-seat hook, an overnight bag with toiletries, four or five changes of underwear, a half-dozen pair of identical dark blue socks, a couple of rolled-up neckties.

A nylon sports bag in the trunk held two hundred thousand dollars and change.

Chapter Two

Two days earlier, I'd been sitting on my porch with the dregs of a rabbit stew. Not that I hunted, but my neighbor Nathan did. Nathan had lived in a cabin up here for better than sixty years. Everyone said set foot on his land, expect buckshot, but right after I moved in he showed up with a bottle of homemade. We sat out here sharing it silently, and ever since, every few weeks, Nathan turns up. Always brings a bottle, sometimes a brace of squirrels so freshly killed they still have that earth-and-copper blood smell, a bundle of quail, a duck or rabbit.

I'd grown up with relatives much like Nathan. We'd see them once or twice a year maybe. On a Sunday, pack ourselves into the cream-over-green Dodge with green plastic shades above the windshield and forward of the wing windows, and drive along narrow highways that let onto blacktop roads flanked on either side by cotton fields, bolls white and surprising as popcorn, sometimes a biplane dipping to spew double barrels of insecticide; then down dirt roads to a rutted offload by Madden Bay where pickups and empty boat trailers sat waiting, and where Louis or Monty would wave as he throttled down the outboard coming into shore, finally kill it and, paddle tucked under an armpit, tracing figure eights, ease the boat back to ground.

What freedom the boat gave up then.

Louis or Monty as well, I think.

I never knew quite what to say to them. They were kind men, tried their best to engage my brother and myself, to care about us and take care to show they did, but the simple truth is that they were as uncomfortable with us as with these towns sprung up all about them, this bevy of decision makers, garbage collectors, bills and liens. I suspect that Louis and Monty may have felt a greater kinship with the bass and bream they pulled mouths gaping from the bay than with Thomas or me. Deep at the center of themselves, my uncles longed for outposts, frontiers, forests, and badlands.

Your own penchant for living at the edge, could it have derived from them? my psychiatric training prompted— silent companion there beside me on the porch, though not as silent as I'd have wished. One of many things I had thought to leave behind when I came here.

The stew was delicious. I'd hacked up the rabbit, put it in a Dutch oven to brown with coarse salt and pepper rubbed in, then added a dash of the leftover from one of Nathan's bottles, carrots and celery and some fresh greens, covered the whole thing, and turned the flame low as I could.

Val had left around midnight. Not only was she uncannily attuned to my need for solitude, she shared that need. We'd been working on her house earlier, came back here afterwards, where I'd set the stew on to simmer as we porched ourselves and sat talking about nothing much at all, clocking the barometer-like fall of whiskey in a bottle of Glenfiddich as the thrum of cicada and locust built towards twilight, then receded. Birds dipped low over the lake, rose against a sky like a basket of abstract fruit: peach, plum, grape-fruit pink.

"Third session in court on a custody case," Val replied when I asked about her day. Legal counsel for the state barracks, she maintained a private practice in family law as well. "Mother's a member of the Church of the Old God."

"Some kind of cult?"

"Close enough. Claim to have returned to the church as it began, in biblical times. Think Baptists or Church of Christ in overdrive."

"I'd rather not."

"Right… The father's a teacher. Medieval history at university level."

"Given the era and perspective, those must be interesting classes."

"I suspect they are, yes."

"How old is the girl?"

"I didn't say it was a girl."

"My guess."

"She's thirteen. Sarah."

"What does *she* want?"

Val snagged the bottle, poured another inch and a half of single malt for both of us.

"What do we all want at that age? Everything."

Dark had fallen. Dead silent now—broken by the call of a frog from down on the lake.

"Smelling good in there." Val lifted her glass, sighting the moon through it as though the glass were a sextant. Find your position, plot your course. "She'll wind up with the mother, I suspect."

"You're representing the father?"

She nodded. "Even though Sarah's where my heart lies."

"Given the circumstances, she must have… what do you call it? a court-appointed advocate, a spokesman?"

"Guardian ad litem, but more a guardian pro forma, I'm afraid, in this case."

Taking my glass with its dreg of Glenfiddich along,

I went in to check on our dinner. It would be better tomorrow, but it was ready now. I pulled out bowls and ladled rabbit stew with barley and thick-cut carrots into them, laid slices of bread atop.

Outside, Val and I sat scooping up steaming spoonfuls and blowing across them.

"It's a messy system," Val said after a blistering mouthful, sucking air. "All kinds of slippage built into it."

"Slippage you can use, though."

I was remembering Sally Gene, a social worker back in Memphis. The whole thing just kind of grew, Sally Gene told me, this whole system of child protection and the laws supporting it—the way people'll take a trailer and keep adding on to it, a porch here, a spare room. No real planning. So half of it's about to fall down around you, none of the doors close, stuff flies in and out of the windows at will. You can use that—but it can also use you. It can use you right up.

"Exactly," Val said. "And a lot of what I manage to accomplish has more to do with slippage than with law. You're standing there before a judge, you *think* you understand the situation, think you know the law and have made a case, but whatever that judge says decides it. Should one man or woman have that much power? Finally you're just hoping the judge slept well, didn't get pissed off at his own kids over the breakfast table."

We ate, then Val, miming a beggar's plea for alms,

held out her bowl. I refilled mine as well and came back onto the porch, screen door banging behind. Immediately Val began dunking the bread, letting it drip.

"Always so dainty. Such manners."

She stuck out her tongue. I pointed to the corner of my mouth to indicate she had food there. She didn't.

"So often there's just no right answer, no solution," she said. "We always insist there has to be. Need to believe that, I guess."

Neither of us spoke for a time then. Spooky cry of an owl from a nearby tree.

"You know, this may be the best thing I've ever eaten. We should have a moment of silence for the rabbit."

"Who gave his life…"

"I can't imagine it was voluntary. Though the image of Mr. Rabbit knocking at Nathan's back door and offering himself up for the better good is an intriguing one."

Finished, she set the bowl on the floor beside her chair.

"Sarah's lost," she said. "Nothing I can do about it. Life with her mother will warp her incontrovertibly. Her father is barely functional. Dresses in whatever's to the left in his closet and through the month moves steadily right, has his CDs numbered and plays them in order. Books on his shelves are arranged by size."

"Maybe she'll save herself."

"Maybe. Some of us do, don't we? It's just others that we can never save."

Within the hour I saw Val to her car. Knew she wouldn't stay but asked anyway. She pulled me close and we stood in silent embrace. That embrace and the warmth of her body, not to mention the silence, seemed answer enough just then to any questions the world might throw me. From the rooftop a barn owl, perhaps the one we'd heard earlier, looked on.

"Fabulous dinner," she said.

"Fabulous companion."

"Yes. You are."

Owl and I watched as the Volvo backed out to begin the long swing around the lake and away. Owl then swiveled his head right around, 180 degrees, like a gun turret. As the sound of Val's motor racketed off the water, I remembered listening to Lonnie's Jeep as it came around the lake that first time. I'd put a spray of iris in the trunk where Val kept her briefcase and enjoyed thinking of her finding the flowers there.

Bit of Glenfiddich left in the bottle, meanwhile.

I poured as the owl flew off to be about its business. This Scotch was mine, and I was going to be about it.

I'd been close to two years on the streets when I came awake in a white room, hearing beeps and a soughing as of pumps close by, garbled conversation further away, ringing phones. I tried to sit up and couldn't. A matronly face appeared above me.

"You've been shot, Officer. You're fine now. But you need to rest."

Her hand rose to the IV beside me and thumbed a tiny wheel there—as I sank.

When next I came around, a different face loomed above me, peering into my eyes from behind a conical light.

"Feeling better, I hope?"

Male this time, British or Australian accent.

Next he moved to the foot of my bed, prodded at my feet. Checking for pulses, as I later learned. He made some notations on a clipboard, set it aside, and reached towards the IV.

I grabbed hold of his hand, shook my head.

"Doctor's orders," he said.

"The doctor's here?"

"Not at the moment, mate."

"He's not, and we are. But he's still making decisions for both of us?"

"You're refusing medication?"

"Do I need it?"

"You have to tell me."

"That I refuse?"

"Yes. So I can chart it."

"Okay, I refuse medication."

"Right you are, then." He picked up the clipboard, made another notation. "Surgeons here like to keep their patients snowed the first twenty-four to thirty-six hours. Some of the nurses question that, and rightly so. But who are we?"

"Besides the ones at bedside going through this shit with us, you mean."

"That's exactly what I mean."

"How long have I been here?"

"Came in around six, p.m. that is, not long before my shift started. That's to intensive care, mind you. You were in OR before, I'd guess an hour or so, started off in ER. They wouldn't have kept you down there long with a GSW, you being police and all."

"What's your name?"

"Ion."

Dawn nibbled at the window.

"Do you know what happened to me, Ion?"

"Shot on duty's what I got at report, just back from OR, standard ICU orders, no complications. Always anxious to get home to her young husband, Billie is. Hold on a sec. I'll get the chart, we can sort this out."

He was back in moments. Phones rang incessantly at the nurse's station outside my door. There must have been an elevator shaft close by. I kept hearing the deep-throated whine of the elevator's voyage, the thunk of it coming into port, the shift in hallway sounds when the doors opened.

Ion pulled a molded plastic visitor's chair up beside the bed, went rummaging through the chart.

"Looks as though you responded to a domestic dispute called in by neighbors. Got there and found a man beating his wife with a segment of garden hose. You took him down—"

"From behind, with a choke hold."

"Oh?"

"And the wife shot me."

"Coming back to you, is it?"

"Not really. But I know how these things usually go."

Perfunctory rap at the door, around the sill of which a face then leant. Young woman with something very close to a Marine buzz cut and a diamond stud in her nose.

"That time already?" Ion said. "Be right with you, C.C. Just give me a minute.

"Shift change," he told me, looking back down at the chart. "Here we go… Bullet passed cleanly through your upper thigh, no major vessels involved. There'd have been a lot of blood, I imagine. A couple of major muscle groups got more or less dissected. All put back right, but muscles take an amazing time to forgive you."

"That why I can't move?"

"That would be the restraints. Sorry." Ion unlashed trailing nylon ties from sidebars of the bed, slipped padded cuffs off wrists and ankles. "Seems you reacted poorly to one of the sedatives, hardly uncommon. But all that lot should be well out of your system by now."

The stud-nosed face appeared again in the doorway.

"C.C. What is it, you've a bloody bus to catch? You're here for twelve hours. Go take some vitals, pretend you're a nurse. I'll be along straightaway, just as I said."

I thanked him.

Standing, he pulled up a trouser leg and rapped knuckles at the pinkish leg thereunder, which gave off a hollow sound. "I've been where you are, Officer, right enough. Compliments of Miss Thatcher."

He never showed up beside my bed again. When I asked, I was told that he'd been assigned to another unit, that all the nurses rotated through the various intensive cares.

"How many ICUs are there?"

"Seeks." Six.

"That's a lot of care."

"Is hard world."

Angie was, what, twenty-four? On the other hand, she was Korean—so maybe she did know, from direct experience, how hard the world could be.

I thought I knew, of course. Weeks of physical therapy, weeks of furiously sending messages down the spinal column to a leg that first ignored the signals then barely acknowledged them, weeks of watching those around me—MS patients, people with birth defects, victims of severe trauma or strokes—taught me different. My world was easy.

Four months later, back at work though still on desk duty, I had personally thanked everyone else involved in my medical care, but in trying to track down Ion found that he'd not merely been assigned to another ICU, as I'd been told, but had left the hospital's employ.

Two or three purportedly official calls from Officer Turner at MPD, and I was pulling into the parking lot of an apartment complex in south Memphis. No sign of air conditioning and the mercury pushing ninety degrees, so most of the apartments had doors and windows open, inviting in a nonexistent breeze. Parking lot filled with pickups drooling oil and boxy sedans well past expiration date. The one-time swimming pool had been filled in with cement, the cement painted blue.

I knocked at the door of 1-C. Had in hand a sack of goodies with a gift bow threaded through the paper handles—candy, cookies, cheese and water biscuits, thumb-sized salamis, and summer sausage.

"Whot?" he said as the door opened. Puffy face, sclera gone red. Wearing shorts and T-shirt. The foot on his good leg was bare; a shoe remained on the other.

Van Morrison playing back in the depths. "Tupelo Honey."

"Whot?" he said again.

"You don't remember me, do you?"

"And I should?"

"Officer Turner. Came in with a GSW long about August. You took care of me."

"Sorry, mate. All a blur to me."

Motion behind him became a body moving towards us. Buzzcut blond hair, diamond stud, not much else by way of disguise. Or of clothes, for that matter.

"I just wanted to thank you," I said, passing across the bag. "Forgive me for intruding."

He took the bag and pulled the handles apart to look in. The bow tore away, dropping to the floor.

"Hey! Thanks, man." He stared for a moment at the bow on the floor by my foot. "You take care, okay?"

None of us, I thought later at home, remembering his kindness and concern, thirty straight leg lifts into what amounted to an hour-long regimen, wall slides and step-ups to go, muscles beginning at last to forgive me, *none of us are exempt.*

Chapter Three

The man back in our holding cell, Judd Kurtz, wasn't talking. When we asked him where the money came from, he grinned and gave us his best try at a jailyard stare. The stare just kind of hung there in no-man's-land between close-cropped brown hair and bullish neck.

We made the necessary calls to State. They'd pull down any arrest records or outstanding warrants on Kurtz, run the fingerprints Don Lee took through AFIS. They'd also check with the feds on recent robberies and reports of missing funds. Barracks commander Bailey said he'd get back to us soonest. We woke bank president Stew Daniels so he could put the money in his vault.

"Want me to stay around?" I asked Don Lee. By this time dawn was pecking at the windows.

"No need to. Go home. Get some sleep. Come back this afternoon."

"You're sure?"

"Get out of here, Turner."

Still cool out by the cabin when I reached it, early-morning sunlight skipping bright coins across the lake. Near and far, from ancient stands of oak and cypress, young doves called to one another. Mist clung to the water's surface. I didn't come here for beauty, but it keeps insisting upon pushing its way in. Val's yellow Volvo was under the pecan tree out front. Two squirrels sat on a low limb eyeing the car suspiciously and chattering away. As I climbed out, Val stepped onto the porch with twin mugs of coffee.

"Heard you were back in port, sailor."

"Aye, ma'am."

"And how's the Fairlane?"

"Not bad, once you discount crop dusters trying to land on the hood."

I'd finally broken down and bought a car, from the same old Miss Shaugnessy who rented out her garage to Jimmy Ray, who bought beer for minors. Thing was a tank: you looked out on a hood that touched down two counties over. Miss Shaugnessy'd bought it new almost forty years ago, paying cash, but never quite learned to drive. It had been up on blocks since, less than a hundred miles on the odometer. Lonnie was the one who talked her into selling it to me. Went over with a couple of plate lunches from Jay's covered in aluminum foil and a quart of beer and came back with the keys.

I don't remember too much more about that morning. Val and I sat side by side on the porch on kitchen chairs I'd fished out of the city dump up the road. I told her about Don Lee's latest catch. About the money in the nylon sports bag. Told her I was tired, bone tired, dead tired. Watched sparrows, cardinals, and woodpeckers alight in the trees and bluejays curse them all. A pair of quail ran, heads and shoulders down like soldiers, from brush to brush nearby. A squirrel came briefly onto the porch and sat on haunches regarding us. I think I told Val about the pork chop.

Next thing I know she's beside me on the bed and I'm suddenly awake. No direct sunlight through east or west windows, so most likely the sun's overhead.

"What, you didn't go in to work today?"

"New policy. State employees are encouraged to telecommute one day a week."

"What the hell for?"

"Clean air legislation."

"Someone's been trucking in the other kind?"

"Sorry. Thought you were awake, but obviously you're not quite. I did mention the government, right?"

"See your point."

"You said to wake you around noon. Coffee's almost fresh and Café Val's open for business. Need a menu?"

"Oatmeal."

"Oatmeal? Here I hook up with an older man, expecting to reap the benefits of his life experience —plumb the depths of wisdom and all that—and what I get is oatmeal?"

She did, and I did, and within the hour, following shower, shave, oatmeal breakfast, and a change of clothes, I pulled in by city hall. The Chariot and Don Lee's pickup were still there, along with June's Neon. Blinds were closed.

Those blinds never get closed except at night.

And the door was locked.

If I hadn't been fully awake before, I was now.

I had a key, of course. What I didn't have was any idea where the key might be. Time to rely on my extensive experience as a law-enforcement professional: I kicked the door in. Luckily a decade's baking heat had done its work. On my third try the doorframe around the lock splintered.

Donna, one of two secretaries from the other half of city hall—mayor's office, city clerk, water and sewage departments, the administrative side of things— appeared beside me to say "We have a spare key, you know." Then she glanced inside.

June lay there, shamrock-shaped pool of blood beneath her head, purse still slung over her shoulder. She was breathing slowly and regularly. Bubbles of blood formed and broke in her right nostril with each breath. As on a movie screen I saw her arrive for her shift, surprising them in the act. She'd have keyed the door and come on in. One hand on the .22 that had spilled from her purse when she fell, I imagined. She'd have realized something wasn't right, same as I did.

Two smaller questions to add to the big one, then.

Why was June carrying a gun in her purse?

And was Don Lee already down when she arrived?

He lay on the floor by the door leading back to the storage room and holding cells. A goose egg the color and shape of an overripe Roma tomato hung off the left side of his head. Glancing through the open door I saw the holding cell was empty. Don Lee's eyes flickered as I knelt over him. He was trying to say something. I leaned closer.

"Gumballs?"

He shook his head.

"Goombahs," he said.

Donna meanwhile had put in a call for Doc Oldham, who, as usual, arrived complaining.

"Man can't even be left alone to have his goddamn lunch in peace nowadays. What the hell're you up to now, Turner? This used to be a nice quiet place to live, you know? Then you showed up."

He dropped to one knee beside June. For a moment I'd have sworn he was going to topple. Droplets of sweat, defying gravity, stood on his scalp. He felt for June's carotid, rested a hand briefly on her chest. Carefully supported her head with one hand while palpating it, checking pupils, ears.

"I'm assuming you've already done this?" he said.

"Pupils equal and reactive, so no sign of concussion. No fremitus or other indication of respiratory difficulty. No real evidence of struggle. Someone standing guard at the door's my guess. A single blow meant only to put her down."

Oldham's eyes met mine. We'd both been there too many times.

"Not bad for an amateur, I was about to say. But you're not, are you? So I was about to make myself an asshole. Not for the first time, mind. And, I sincerely hope, not for the last." Grabbing at a tabletop, he wobbled to his feet. "I need to look at the other one?"

"Pupils unequal but reactive. Unconscious now, but he spoke to me earlier and responds to pain. Doesn't look to be any major blood loss. Vitals are good. BP I'd estimate at ninety over sixty, thereabouts."

"Ambulance on the way?"

"Call's in."

"Could take some time. Rory ain't always easy to

rouse, once he's got hisself bedded down for the day.
Damn it all, we're looking at a major goddamn crime
scene here."

"Afraid so."

"Ever tell you how much I hate court days?"

"Once or twice."

"There're those who'd be pleased to pay for your
ticket back home, you know." He leaned heavily
against the wall, reeling down breaths in stages, like a
kite from the sky. "But you ain't going away, are you,
boy?"

"No, sir."

"You sure 'bout that?"

"I am."

He pushed himself away from the wall.

"Good. Things been a hell of a lot more interesting
around here since you came."

Doc Oldham and I packed the two of them off to the
hospital up Little Rock way, then he had to demon-
strate his new step. He'd recently taken up tap dancing,
God help us all, and every time you saw him, he
wanted to show off his latest moves. This from a man
who could barely stand upright, mind you. It was like
watching a half-rotted pecan tree go au point. But
eventually he left to make another try at his goddamn
lunch, and I went to work. I'd barely got started when

Buster arrived. Buster filled in as relief cook at the diner, cleaned up there most nights, snagged whatever other work he could. I never could figure what it was about him, some kind of palsy or just plain old nerves, but some part of Buster always had to be moving.

"Doc says you could use help gettin'th'office cleaned up, " he said, looking around. When his head stopped moving, a foot started. "'Pears to me he was right."

"You don't have to do that."

"Well, no sir, I don't," he said, grinning. Then the lips relaxed and his eyes met mine. A shaky hand rose between us. "Sure enough could use the work, though."

"Twenty sound okay?"

"Yessir. Sounds *right* good. Specially with my anniversary coming up and all."

"How many years does this make for you and Della?"

"Fifty-eight."

"Congratulations."

"She the one deserves congratulations, puttin' up with the likes of me all these years."

Buster went back to the storage room to find what he needed as I sank in again. Buster could clean the stairs at Grand Central Station during rush hour without getting in anyone's way. Someone once said of a

Russian official who survived regime after regime that he'd learned to dodge raindrops and could make his way through a downpour without ever getting wet. That's Buster.

Don's desk tray held his report, with a photocopy of the original speeding ticket stapled to it. In the ledger he'd logged time of arrest, reason for same, time of arrival at the office, booking number. The column for PI (personal items) was checked, as was that for FP (fingerprinted) and PC (phone call).

Just out of curiosity, I paged back to see when we'd last fingerprinted or given a phone call. We rarely had sleepovers, and when we did they were guys who'd had a little too much to drink, bored high school kids caught out vandalizing, the occasional mild domestic dispute needing cool-off time.

Four months back, I'd answered a suspicious person call at the junior high. Dominic Ford had offered no resistance, but I'd brought him in and put his stats in the system on the off chance that he might be a pedophile or habitual offender. Turned out he was an estranged father just trying to get a glimpse of his twelve-year-old daughter, make sure she was okay.

Six months back, Don Lee responded to a call that a man "not from around here" was sitting on the only bench in the tiny park at the end of Main Street talking to himself. Thinking he could be a psychiatric patient, Don Lee printed him. What he was, was minister of a Pentecostal church in far south Memphis, out towards the state border where gambling casinos afloat on the river have turned Tunica into a second Atlantic City. He'd only wanted to get back to the kind of place he grew up, he said. Touch down there, *feel* it again. He'd been sitting on the bench working up his sermon.

The previous entry was for that time, a year ago, when Lonnie, Don Lee, and I discovered how Carl Hazelwood had been killed—the day the sheriff got shot.

All these years, I'd never seen anything remotely resembling a jailbreak and assumed they only happened in old Western or gangster movies. But it was obvious this crew had come here specifically to spring Judd Kurtz. Goombahs, Don Lee had said. Even among the most hardassed, there aren't many who'll step up to a law office, even a far-flung, homespun one like ours, with such impunity.

I sat looking at that tick underneath PC. Then I made my own call, to Mabel at Bell South.

"Don Lee and Miss June gonna be okay?" she said immediately upon hearing my voice.

"We hope so. Meanwhile, I need a favor."

"Whatever I can do."

"How much do you know about what went down over here?"

"Just someone stormed in and beat crap out of the two of them's all I heard."

"That someone came to town to break out a man Don Lee had detained on a traffic violation."

"Take safe driving seriously, do they?"

Known for her biting wit, Mabel was. Not to mention the choicest gossip in town.

"The man made a phone call from this office just after Don Lee booked him in, around one a.m. I know it's—"

"Sure it is. Now ask me if I care. Just give me five, ten minutes."

"Thanks, sweetheart."

"For what? I'm not doing this."

Never mind five or ten minutes, it was more like two.

She read out the number. "Placed at one-fourteen." A Memphis exchange.

"Any way you can check to see what that number is?"

"Like I haven't already? Nino's Restaurant. Two lines. One's the official listing, looks like it gets almost all the calls. The other—"

"Is probably an office or back booth."

"Must be a city thing," Mabel said in the verbal equivalent of a shrug. "That do it for you?"

"I owe you, Mabel."

"You just be sure to give Miss June and Don Lee my best when you see them."

"I will."

"'Scuse me, Mr. Turner?" Head bobbing, Buster stood in the doorway. "'Bout done here. S'posed to go wash the mayor's car now. One or two more besides, I s'pect." When his head went still, an arm rose. "Came upon this back in there."

A business card. I took it. Put a twenty and a ten in its place.

"Much obliged, sir."

"When's your anniversary, Buster?"

"Thursday to come."

"Maybe you could bring Della over to my place that night, let Val and me fix dinner for you both. We'd love to meet her."

"Well now, I'd surely like that, Mr. Turner. 'Preciate the asking. And forgive me for saying it, but Della'd be powerful uncomfortable with that."

"I understand. Maybe some other time."

"Maybe so."

"A shame, though."

"Yessir. It surely is."

Chapter Four

Latter-Day City Constables, we seldom know the out-come of our efforts. We take on the end runs and heavy lifting, fill in paperwork, testify at trials, move on. It's not *Gunsmoke,* not even *NYPD Blue.* Occa-sionally we hear on the grapevine that Shawn DeLee's been sent up for life, or, if we care to check comput-erized records and have time to do so, learn that Billy-boy Davis has been re-renabbed by federal marshals on a fugitive warrant. To others our talk is forever of jus-tice and community standards. Among ourselves it's considerably baser.

I'd been out of the life a long time now. But weeks back, Herb Danziger up in Memphis had somehow tracked me down and called to tell me that Lou Winter, having exhausted appeals, was scheduled for execution.

Danziger was pro bono lawyer for Lou Winter at his initial trial. He'd put in thirty-some years making certain that big rich corporations got bigger and richer, then one day ("No crisis of conscience, I was just bored out of my mind") he gave it up and started taking on, in both senses of the phrase, the hard cases. Another six years of that before an unappeased client stepped out of the doorway of Danziger's apartment house one evening as he returned home. Damndest thing you ever saw, the paramedic who responded said. We get there and this guy is sitting on the sidewalk with his back against the wall and his legs out straight in front of him. There's the handle of a hunting knife sticking out of his head, like he has a horn, you know? And he's singing "Buffalo Gals Won't You Come Out Tonight."

He survived, but with extensive brain damage. His hands shook with palsy and one foot dragged, paving of his memory gone to potholes. He'd been in an assisted-living home ever since. But old cohorts showed up regularly to visit, bringing with them all the latest courthouse gossip.

"Early September is what they're saying. I'll keep you posted."

"Thanks, Herb. You doing okay?"

"Never better. Occupational therapist here would adopt me if she could. Who'd ever have suspected I had artistic talent? My lanyards and decoupage are the best. Others look upon them and weep."

"Anything you need?"

"I'm good, T. You get up this way, just come see me, that's all."

"I'll do that."

Lou Winter had killed four children, all males aged ten to thirteen. Unlike other juvenile predators, he never molested them or was in any way improper. He met them mostly at malls, befriended them, took them out for elaborate meals and often a movie, then killed them and buried them in his backyard. Each grave had a small garden plot above it: tomatoes above one, zucchini above another, Anaheim peppers above a third. From the ground of the most recent, only a short stem with two tiny leaves protruded.

It was my fourth, maybe fifth catch as detective, just a missing-persons case at the time. I'd been kicked upstairs arbitrarily and had little idea what I was doing or how to go about it. Everyone in the house knew that—watch commanders, other detectives, technicians in forensics, patrol, probably the cleaning lady. I was a week into the case with no land in sight when I knocked off around six one night and went out to find a note tucked under my windshield wiper. I never did find out who put it there. It had the name of the missing child on it, the one I was looking for, followed by the number four. It also had another name, and the address of a pet shop at Westwood Mall.

A buzzer sounded faintly as I walked in. Lou Winter came out of the back of the store and stood watching me, knowing even then, I think, who I was. When I told him, he just nodded, eyes still on mine. Something strange about those eyes, I thought even then.

"I have a mother cat giving birth back there," he said. "Can you give me a few minutes?"

I went with him and stood alongside as, cooing and petting, tugging gently with a finger to urge the first kitten out, the first of five, he helped ease her birth. No, not five: six. For, long after the others had dropped into our world, another head began showing.

The last kitten had only one front leg, something wrong with its skull as well. Holding it tenderly, Lou Winter said, "She'll reject it, but we have to try, don't we?" as he pushed the others aside and placed the new one closest to her.

"I'll get my things." A gray windbreaker. A gym bag containing, I would learn later, toothbrush and tooth-paste, a Red Chief notebook and a box of Number 2 pencils, several washcloths, six pair of white socks still in paper bands, a pocket-size paperback Bible. "I'll just lock up." Taking a cardboard sign off a hook alongside, "Back in a Jiff," he hung it on the door. "Marcie comes in after gym practice. Be here any minute now."

He never asked how I found him, never showed any surprise.

Once we'd left the store, I noticed, he began to seem awkward or uncertain, staying close to me, face bunched in concentration. Macular degeneration, I'd learn later. Like many whose faculties decay slowly, he had compensated, memorizing his surroundings, working out ways to function. But Lou Winter was more than half blind.

Outside the station house, a man in an expensive suit and shoes that cost about the same as the suit stepped up and introduced himself as Mr. Winter's lawyer. He and Winter regarded one another a moment, then Winter nodded.

And that was Herb Danziger.

Years later, after we'd got to be friends of a sort, I asked Herb how he happened to show up that day. "I was tipped off," he said. "An anonymous phone call." Then, smiling, added: "You don't think a man's own lawyer would turn him in, do you?"

Inside, waving aside Danziger's caution and counsel, Lou Winter told us everything. The four children, what they'd eaten together, movies they'd seen, the gravesites. Dr. Vandiver, a psychiatrist who did consulting work for the department, came over from Baptist there towards the end. "What do you think, Doctor?" Captain Adams asked. Vandiver went on staring out the window. "I've been trying to put it into words," he said after a moment. "The word I keep coming up with is *sadness.*"

It took the jury less than thirty minutes to come back with a verdict and the judge all of two to sentence Lou Winter to death. Herb Danziger carried on appeal after appeal in Winter's name, right up to the day of his assault. He'd even tried to represent him once afterwards. But when his time came, Herb sat there watching the blades on the ceiling fan go round and round, intrigued by the shadows they made. The judge put off proceedings till the following week and appointed a new attorney.

I hung up the phone after talking to Herb. Clouds moved along the sky as though, having misspoken, they were in a hurry to get offstage. Across the street Terry Billings's legs stuck out from beneath his pickup as he worked on his transmission for the third time this month, trying to wring out yet another few hundred miles.

I was thinking about Herb, about Lou Winter, and remembering what Dr. Vandiver had so untypically said.

Sadness.

Not for himself, but for the others, the children. Or for all of us. In some strange manner, Lou Winter was connected to humanity as few of us are, but the connection had gone bad. Small wires were broken, sparks dribbled out at joins.

Once I had wanted nothing more than to see Lou Winter convicted, then executed. I understood why Herb held on: in a world all too rapidly emptying itself of Herb's presence, Lou was one of the few tangible links to his past, to what his life had stood for, what he had made of it.

Was it really any different for me?

Lou Winter had been a part of my life and world for as long. It was altogether possible that in losing him I would be losing some unexplored subcontinent of my self

That same day, I remember, I stopped Gladys Tate for driving drunk. She was in husband Ed's '57 Chevy and almost fell twice getting out. She'd already run into something and smashed the headlight and half the grille. When I mentioned that Ed was going to be damned mad, she grinned with one side of her face, winked with the other, and said, "Ed won't care. He's got a new toy." His new toy was a woman he met at the bowling alley up by Poplar Grove, the one he'd left town with. Gladys looked off at the old church, now mostly jagged, gaping boards and yellowed white paint, though a skeletal steeple still stood. Then her eyes swam back to mine. "My clothes are in the dryer," she said, "can I go home soon?"

Chapter Five

The business card was for a financial consultant in offices just off Monroe in Memphis. That consultant thing had always eluded me, I could never understand it. As society progresses, we move further and further away from those who actually do the work. Consulting, I figured, was about as far as one could get before launching oneself into the void.

I came here with clear purpose. I'd be on my own, no attachments, no responsibility. Now I look around and find myself at the center of this community, so much so that freeing myself for a few days in Memphis took some doing.

First call was to Lonnie. Sure, he'd fill in, no problem. Be good to be back in harness, long as he knew it was short-term.

"I'll try to keep it down to a minimum," I said.

"You're going after them, aren't you?"

"You wouldn't?"

"They hurt my daughter, Turner. For no good reason save she was there."

"Figure they can do whatever they want out here on the edge, I'm thinking."

"That's what they're thinking too. Just don't forget to give the local force a courtesy call."

"I'm not sure MPD wants to hear from me."

"Call them anyway. You still have any contacts there?"

"Tell the truth, I don't know."

"Find out. And if you do, cash them in for whatever they're worth. Nickel, dime—whatever."

Next call was to barracks commander Bailey, who pledged to send down a couple of retired state troopers to rotate shifts as deputies. "Believe me, they'll appreciate the chance to get out of the house."

Then Val.

"Let me guess. You're going to be away for a while." She laughed. "Commander Bailey told me." She was counsel for the barracks, after all. "Have to admit it came as no surprise. Any idea when you'll be back?"

"I'll call, let you know."

"You better."

"I'll miss you."

Another rapid burst of the laughter I had come so

to treasure. "It's pitiful," she said, "how much I hoped you might say something like that."

Forty minutes later I was heading up Highway 51 in the Chariot, Lonnie's Jeep, with an overnight bag of underwear and socks, two shirts, spare khaki pants just in case, basic toiletries. The gun I never carried, a .38 Police Special Don Lee insisted on providing me when I started working with him, lay swaddled in a hand towel, in a quart Glad bag, under the passenger seat. I imagined that I could feel it pulling at me from there, a gravity I was loath to give in to or admit.

I hadn't been back to Memphis in, what, close to two years? At some essential level it never seems to change much. More fast-food franchises and big-box stores pop up, the streets continue to crumble from center to sides, there are ever-longer stretches of abandoned shops, businesses, entire office buildings. When the economy goes bad, the first leaks spring at the weakest segments. The Delta's been hard hit for decades. You cruise the main street in small towns like Helena, just down the river a piece, or over by Rosedale, half the stores are empty as old shoes. The river's still impressive, but it ceased offering much by way of economic advantage long ago.

Just inside the city limits, I stopped at Momma's Café for coffee and a burger. Place was all but hidden behind a thicket of service trucks and hard-ridden pickups. Even here in the South, central cities become ever more homogeneous, one long stuttering chain of McDonald's and KFC and Denny's, while local cafés and restaurants cling to the outskirts as though thrown there by centrifugal force. Nowadays I find I have to lower myself into the city environment, any city environment, by degrees, like a diver with bends coming up—but I'm going down. And Momma's was just right for it. From there I drove on in and dragged for a couple of hours the streets I used to run as a cop, feeling the city slowly fall into place around me. Drove north on Poplar where East High School once stood, now a nest of cozy aluminum-sided single-family dwellings with tiny manicured lawns front and back. Drove by Overton Square. Cruised down Walnut, took the left at Vance and crossed Orleans. Hit Able and proceeded north past Beale and Union. Swung by 102-A Birch Street where I'd shot my partner Randy.

When I worked out of it, Central Precinct was on South Flicker, second floor of the old Armor Station. Now it was housed at 426 Tillman in the Binghamton section, for many years a hard and hard-bitten part of the city that looked to be, especially with the recent completion of Sam Cooper Boulevard just north, on its way back.

I pulled into a visitor space, went in and gave my name and credentials to a sergeant at the front desk, who said someone would be with me directly. *Directly*, I surmised, here meant something on the order of *any day now* back home. Eventually Sergeant Collins came out from behind his desk and escorted me through a reef of battered metal desks to an office at the rear.

Sam Hamill had been a rookie along with me. Now, heaven help him, he was Major Hamill, the watch commander. Forty pounds heavier than back in the day, a lot less hair, deltas of fat deposits around the eyes. Wearing a navy gabardine suit and a charcoal knit tie that would have been the bee's knees circa 1970.

"Turner. Good Lord."

"Never know who or what's likely to walk into a police station, do you?"

He came up from behind the desk to shake my hand. Took some effort. Definitely the coming up from behind the desk. Probably, too, in another way, shaking my hand.

"So how the hell've you been?"

"Away."

He eased himself back into his chair in a manner that brought hemorrhoids or getting shot in the butt to mind. "So I heard. Guys that told me, it was like, 'Hey, he's gone. Let's celebrate.'"

"Don't doubt it for a minute."

We sat regarding one another across the archipelago of his desk.

"You fucked up bad on the job, Turner."

"Not just on the job."

"What I heard." He stared, smiled and wheezed a bit before saying, "So where've you been?"

"Home, more or less."

"And now you're back."

"Briefly. Touching down. Here and gone before you know it."

"I was just on the phone with Lonnie Bates."

"Guess that explains why Sergeant Collins at the desk had me cooling my heels."

"Sheriff Bates speaks well of you. Seems a good man."

"He is. Would have made a great con artist. People tend to see him as just this hicktown officer, and he plays up to it, when the truth is, he's as smart and as capable as anyone I've ever worked with. Same goes for his deputy."

"Other deputy, you mean."

"Other deputy, right."

Sam nodded. When he did, cords of loose skin on his neck writhed. "Bates told me what happened."

He fiddled with a Webster cup. Clutch of ballpoint pens, letter opener, scissors, six-inch plastic ruler, couple of paper-sheathed soda straws, a cheap cigar in its wrapper.

"Deputy sheriff from another county won't hold much water here in Memphis."

"I know that. On the other hand, I do have a fugitive warrant."

"So Sheriff Bates informed me. So after I hung up from talking to him, I called over to our own sheriff's office and spoke with the fugitive squad there, people you'd ordinarily be expected to coordinate with. We help them out sometimes. Game of 'Mother May I?' is mostly what it is. You know how it works."

I nodded. "They give you permission to take one giant step?"

"So happens they did."

"Your town, Sam, and your call. Just I'd appreciate being there."

"Course, first we have to figure out where *there* is."

"Judd Kurtz doesn't ring any bells?"

"Not with me. Nino's we know. Also Semper Fi Investments. We keep an eye out. Hang on a minute."

He punched in an interoffice number, waited a couple of rings.

"Hamill. Any word on the street about a missing quarter-mill or so?… I see… Say I was to whisper the name Judd Kurtz in your ear, would it get me a kiss?… Thanks, Stan."

He hung up.

"Stan heads up our task force on organized crime. Says a week or two back, a minor leaguer made his rounds—passed the collection plate, as Stan put it—

then went missing. Rumor has it he's a nephew to one of the bosses. Stan also says someone's tried his best to put a lid on it."

"But even the best lids leak."

Sam nodded.

"Stan have any idea where we can find this supposed nephew?"

"You really been away that long, Turner? You think we're gonna find this guy? What, he ripped off one of the bosses, then got himself arrested in the boondocks, made them send in the thick-necks? Those sound like career moves to you? Nephew or not, he's under Mud Island by now."

"In which case I need to find the thick-necks."

"How did I know?" Eyes went to the window looking out into the squad room. All the good stuff happened out there. He used to be out there himself. "You know your warrant doesn't cover them."

"I'm not asking you to help me, Sam. Just hoping you and your people won't get in my way."

"Oh, I think we can do a little better than that."

Again he punched in a number. "Tracy, you got a minute?"

Ten, twelve beats and the door opened.

Thirtyish, button jeans, dark T-shirt with a blazer over, upturned nose, silver cuffs climbing the rim of one ear.

"Tracy Caulding, Deputy Sheriff Turner. Believe it

or not, this man used to be one of ours. The two of us came on the job together, in fact."

"Wow. Now *there's* a recommendation."

"Back home, his sheriff got taken down by some of our local hardcases. Turner would like to meet them."

"Taken down?"

"He's alive. Badge is gonna spend some time in the drawer, though."

"That really blows."

"No argument from me. City rats gone country, Tracy. It's not their territory, what the fuck? They're in, they're out, they're gone."

"Where am I in this, Sam?"

"You ever said 'sir' or 'boss' your whole life?"

"Not as I recall. My mother—"

"Was a hardcore feminist, six books, whistle-blower on the evils of society. I do read personnel files, Tracy."

She smiled, quite possibly in that moment adding to global warming.

"Thing is, Turner here's been away a while. We don't want him getting lost. Show him around, help facilitate his reentry."

"Ride shotgun is what you mean," Tracy Caulding said.

"I don't need protection, Sam."

"I know you don't, old friend. What I'm thinking is, with you back, maybe *we* do."

Chapter Six

Had a wonderful barbeque dinner that night, Tracy Caulding and I, at Sonny Boy's #2 out on Lamar: indoor picnic benches, sweaty plastic pitchers of iced tea, roll of paper towels at each table. There was no Sonny Boy's #1, Tracy told me—not that, after a bite or two, anyone was likely to care. Amazing, blazing pork, creamy cool cole slaw, butterbeans and pinto beans baked together, biscuits. "Biscuits fresh ever hour," according to a hand-lettered sign.

For all its cultural razing, Memphis remains one of the great barbeque towns.

Tracy lowered a stand of ribs she'd sucked dry onto her plate and, tearing off a panel of paper towel, wiped her mouth as lustily as she'd taken to the barbeque. She picked up another segment of ribs, held it poised for launch, told me: "Stan Dimitri and I had coffee together this afternoon. From organized crime? He filled me in on the Aleché network."

"That what they're calling them now? Networks? To us they were just gangs."

"Then for a while it went to crews. Now it's networks. This one's responsible for much of the money that gets dry-cleaned through Semper Fi Investments. Run by, if you can believe it, a Native American who passes himself off as some sort of Mediterranean. Born Jimmy McCallum, been going by Jorge Aleché for years now."

"He the one with the nephew?"

"Stan thinks so."

"Stan thinks—that's the best you have?"

Shrugging. "What can I say?"

"Well… What I think is, it's time for a massive rattling of the cage."

The second portion of ribs dropped onto her plate. A third or fourth paper towel wiped away sins of the immediate past. Older sins took a bit longer.

"And here Sam thinks you're out of touch." She held up her beer, tipping its neck towards me. "I know who you are, Turner."

"I'd be surprised if you didn't. However big the city, the job's always a small town."

"I started hearing stories about you the day I first hit the streets."

"And I remember the first time I looked in a car's rearview mirror and saw the legend 'Objects May Be Closer Than They Appear.'"

"What the fuck's *that* mean?"

"That you can't trust stories."

"Yeah, but how many of us ever get to have stories told about us?" She drained her beer. "You notice how these bottles keep getting smaller?"

From the breast pocket of her blazer she took a narrow reporter's notebook. Found a free page, scribbled addresses and phone numbers, tore the page off and passed it me.

"Consider it part of your orientation package."

"You memorized all this?"

"Some people have trick joints, like their thumbs bend back to their forearms? I have a trick memory. I hear something, see something, I've got it forever."

"Buy you another beer before the bottles get too small? Alcohol kills brain cells, you know—could help wean you off that memory thing."

"Worth a try."

I got the waiter's attention, ordered another beer for Tracy, bourbon straight up for myself. He brought them and began clearing plates.

"Speaking of stories, I remember one I read years ago," Tracy said. "I was into science fiction then, and new to reading. Every book I opened was a marvel.

One of the older writers—Kuttner, Kornbluth, those guys. People lived almost forever. But every hundred years or so they had to come back to this center where they'd plunge into this pool and swim across it. To rejuvenate them, I'm sure the story pointed out. Symbol of rebirth. But what I got from it was how the water of that miraculous pool would take away their memories, wipe them clean, let them go on."

I took a fond, measured sip of my bourbon. There was a time in my life when measured sips hadn't been called for. That whole measurement thing creeps up on us. Start off counting hairs in the bathtub drain, before we know it we're telling people we're only allowed a cup and a half of coffee a day, reading labels for saturated-fat content, trying to portion out our losses, like a double-entry accountant, to history and failing memory.

"I'm not sure I know how to respond," I told Tracy.

"Yeah. Me either. Exactly what I mean. Four hundred killed when the roof of a substandard apartment building collapses in Pakistan. A fifteen-year-old goes into his high school with an assault weapon and kills three teachers, the principal, twelve fellow students. Half the citizens of some country you never heard of go after the other half, kill or butcher them and bulldoze them into mass graves. There's a proper response to something like that? You get to wishing you could go for a swim, wipe it all away. But you can't."

We tossed off the remainder of our drinks in silence and called it a night. Enough of the world's eternal problems and our own.

"Check in tomorrow?" Tracy said.

"First thing."

"Where are you staying?"

Since I was here on my own dime, I'd taken the cheapest room I could find, at Nu-Way Motel on the city's outer rings. Each unit was painted a different pastel shade, mine what I could only think of as Pepto-Bismol pink. A stack of fifties magazines inside would not have surprised.

Walking Tracy Caulding to her blue Honda Civic, I gave her my location, room and phone number. "No need to write them down for you's my guess," I said, getting another glimpse of the smile that had lit up Sam's office back at the station. From habit I looked in to clear the car, saw a ziggurat of textbooks on the back seat.

"What's this? Not a dedicated law officer?"

She held up her hands, palm out, in mock surrender. "Got me dead to rights."

"Graduate school, from the look of it."

"I confess. M.A. in social work, six credits to go."

She leaned back against the rear door, tugging at the silver-cuffed ear.

"Cop was the last thing I thought I'd be. From the time I was eleven, twelve years old, I was going to be a teacher. Nose forever in a book and all that. But I grew up in a trailer park, no way my parents could afford even local colleges. I had grand ambitions, though, applied all over the mid-South, even places like Tulane and Duke. Memphis State came through with a full scholarship. I had a job teaching sixth grade promised before I'd even graduated. Five weeks in, I walked away from it."

She put her hand on my arm.

"Everything I'd taken for granted all those years was gone. I had no idea who I was, what I could do, and I had to work. Of a Sunday morning I was reading want ads when one at the very corner of the page caught my eye. Police badge to the left. Have a degree? it said. Want to make a difference?—or something equally lame. Another of the department's periodic thrusts to improve its image. Wanted people with degrees, offered an accelerated training program for those who quali-fied. So here I am. Telling you way more than you wanted to know. Sorry."

"Don't be."

She was in the car now, looking out.

"We should talk about counseling and social work sometime," I said.

"Did a bit of it yourself, from what I hear."

"More like I muddied the water."

"So we should. Just don't tell me I'm wrong, okay?" Hauling her seat belt across. "See you tomorrow, Turner." Face in the rearview mirror as she drove away. Objects may be closer than they appear.

Back at the motel I punched my way through a thicket of numbers, 9 for an outside line, 1 for long distance, area code, credit-card number, personal code. Quite the modern lawman.

"Sheriff's office."

"Who's speaking?"

"Rob Olson."

"Trooper?"

"You bet. Who's this?"

"Turner, up in Memphis."

"The deputy, right?"

"Right. Don't guess Lonnie'd be around this late, would he?"

"He's always around. Though it might be best if you didn't tell him I said that." Miles and miles away, coffee got slurped. "Be here right this minute save he's out to an accident. Told him I'd go but he wouldn't hear of it. You hold a minute, Turner? Got someone on the other line."

Then he was back.

"That's Bates on line two. He's at the hospital with an accident victim, wants to speak with you. Hold on,

I'll try to transfer you."

Some time went by.

"Turner. You there? I can't get this damn thing to work. And I think I just hung up on the sheriff. He's still over to the hospital. You wanta call him there?"

He gave me the number, and I did.

"Those boys at the barracks are the best you'll see at paperwork," Lonnie said when I told him what happened. "Other things…"

Someone was there by him, complaining. I'd probably called in to the ER nurse's station, which might be the only line functioning this time of night. The local hospital wasn't a hell of a lot larger or more complicated than our office.

"Official police work," he said. "Chill, Gladys." Then to me: "So you're still in Memphis. Any action?"

I filled him in on my visit. Connecting with Sam Hamill, meeting Tracy. Think I may have found out where to go to get what I'm looking for, I told him.

"That's good. Quick."

"I followed your advice."

"Hamill put you and Tracy together knowing she'd give up the contact, he wouldn't have to." As always, Lonnie was a move ahead.

"Way I saw it, too."

"So why the fancy footwork?"

"Maybe they figure I can take care of a problem

they haven't been able to."

Lonnie was silent for a moment.

"In which case, since Hamill laid out the official face of the thing for you, even assigned an officer, the MPD can in no way be held responsible. Either you handle it and you're home before anyone knows better—"

"Or I get, as our British friends say, nicked for the deed, in which case Sam and the MPD disclaim to their heart's content."

"Clean."

"More than one way to get the job done."

"Always. Damn! Now the goddamned beeper's going off. Hang on."

I heard voices behind, just out of range of intelligibility.

"Shirley checking in," Lonnie said moments later.

"You've got a beeper now."

"Simon has a band concert tomorrow, some kind of solo. Wife wanted to be sure I would make it, gave me hers." Simon in buzzcut and baggies was the older of two sons. The younger, Billy, despite the flag of multiple piercings, had no direction any of us could discern but was a sweetheart, maybe the closest thing to an innocent human being I've known.

"How's June?"

"Cleared by her doctors and home with us. Mostly herself, but sometimes it's like she's not really there, she's gone off someplace else."

"Not surprising, with what she's just been through."

"I hope."

"Give it time. Don Lee?"

"Stable, they keep telling me—though he hasn't come round yet. Wait and see, they say, we just have to wait and see."

Gladys was back, loudly demanding return of the phone he'd taken hostage. Lonnie ignored her.

"Trooper said you wanted to talk to me. What's up?"

"May be nothing to it, but the accident I answered the call to?"

"Yes?"

"It got called in as a collision, but what happened was, Madge Gunderson passed out at the wheel and ran into a tree."

"Madge okay?" Madge had been a not-so-secret drinker most of her life. Her husband Karel died last year, and since then, maybe from grief, maybe from the fact that she didn't have to hide it anymore, the drinking had kind of got out of control.

"She will be. Just some gashes and the like. Looked worse than it is. This happened out on State Road 419. Woman driving behind her saw the whole thing, called it in on a cell phone."

"Okay."

"Woman's from up Seattle way, just passing through.

I thanked her, naturally, took her statement. Then she says, 'You're the sheriff?' and when I say, 'Right now I am , she asks does a man named Turner work with me."

"Say what she wanted?"

"Not a word. Sat there smiling at her and waiting, all she did was smile back."

"What's she look like?"

"Late twenties, early thirties, light brown hair cut short, five-eight, one-thirty. Easy on the eye, as my old man would of said. Jeans and sweatshirt, kind with a hood, ankle-high black Reeboks."

"Name?"

"J. T. Burke. That's Burke with an e, and just the initials."

No one I knew. Maybe a patient from my days as a counselor, was my first thought. Though it was doubtful any patient could have traced me here, or would have reason to.

"Don't suppose she said where she was headed."

"Gave me that same smile when I asked."

"That it, then?"

"Pretty much."

"So give Gladys back her phone already."

In exchange I gave him the name and location of my motel and my phone number, told him to call if he had any updates on Don Lee or happened to hear again from Ms. Burke.

Chapter Seven

Couldn't sleep.

Out on the streets at 2 a.m. looking for an open restaurant. Back to city habits that quickly. Had my book, just needed light, coffee, maybe a sandwich. Do the Edward Hopper thing.

Dino's Diner, half a mile in towards the city proper. "Open 24 hours" painted on the glass in foot-high blue letters. Also "Daily Specials" and "Hearty Breakfasts." These in yellow.

"Getchu?" the waitress, Jaynie, said, handing over a much-splattered menu. "T'drink?"

Coffee. Definitely.

And received a reasonable facsimile of same, though it took some time. Peak hour, after all. Had to be three or four other patrons at least.

"Two scrambled, bacon, grits, biscuit," I told Jaynie

when my coffee came.

Eggs were rubber—no surprise there—bacon greasy and underdone, biscuit from a can. Here I am in the Deep South and I get a canned biscuit? On the other hand, the grits were amazing.

The book also disappointed. Three refills and I was done with it, wide margins, large type, pages read almost as quickly as I turned them. Novels tend to be short these days. Probably most of them should be even shorter. This one was about a doctor, child of the sixties and long a peace activist, who goes after the men who raped and killed his wife and disposes of them one by one. Title: *Elective Surgery.*

I took out my wallet, unfolded the notebook page Tracy Caulding had given me. Three addresses, none of which meant much to me. A lot of Lanes and Places, bird names the rage. Meadowlark Drive, Oriole Circle, like that. But just then a cab pulled up out front and the driver came in. Jaynie slapped a cup of coffee down before him without being asked. He was two stools away. One of those in-betweens you find all over the South, darkish skin, could be of Italian descent, Mediterranean, Caribbean, Creole. Fine features, a broad nose, gold eyes—like a cat's. Wearing pleated khakis with enough starch to have held on to their crease though now well crumpled about the crotch, navy blue polo shirt, corduroy sport coat.

I caught his eye, asked "How's it going?"

"Been better. Been worse, too."

"And will be again."

"Believe it."

He pulled out a pack of Winstons, shook one loose and got it going. Then as an afterthought glanced my way, took the pack out again and offered me one. When I declined, he put the cigarettes back, held out his hand. We shook.

"Danel. Like Daniel without the i."

"Turner... Any chance you could help me with these?"

I slid the paper across. After a moment he looked up.

"From out of town, are you."

I pled guilty.

"But you have business here." He tapped at the paper.

"Yes."

"Well, sir, this here ain't part of Memphis at all, it's another country. Birdland, some of us call it. Bunch of whitebread castles's what it is. Some Johnny-come-lately builds him a house, next Johnny comes along and has to outdo him, build a bigger one. Kind of business that gets transacted out there, most people'd do best to stay away from. I'm guessing you're not most people."

"Can you give me directions?"

"Yeah, sure, I could do that. Or—" He threw back

his coffee. "What the hell, it's a slow night, I'll run you out there."

We struck a deal. I picked up the Chariot as he sat idling in the Nu-Way Motel parking lot, then pulled in behind and followed him to city's edge. Here be dragons. We'd been cruising for close to thirty minutes, I figured, six or seven classics on whatever station I'd found by stabbing the Seek button—Buffalo Spring-field ("There's some-thing hap-pen-ing here…"), Bob Seger's "Night Moves"—when Danel pulled his Checker cab onto the shoulder, a wide spot intended for rest stops, repairs, tire changes. I came alongside and we wound down windows.

"Here's where I bail," he said. "Place you're looking for's just around that bend. Don't be lookin' for the welcome mat to be out. Ain't the kind to be expecting company up in there."

I hoped not.

"Good luck, man."

"Thanks for your help." I'd paid him back at the diner. He had a good night.

"You're welcome. Prob'ly ain't done you no favor, though."

I pulled back onto the road, along the curve, cut the engine to coast into a driveway inhabited by a black BMW and a gussied up red Ford pickup, chrome pipes, calligraphic squiggle running from front fender to rear wheel well, driver's-side spotlight. Backed out then and parked the jeep a quarter-mile up the road, at another of those pull-offs.

The house was a castle, all right—like something imagined by Dr. Seuss. Classic middle-American tacky. Once in El Paso I'd seen a huge bedroom unit that looked to be marble but, when you touched it, turned out to be thin plastic. It was like that.

In the front room just off the entryway (as I peered through what I could only think of as eight-foot-tall wing windows) a large-screen TV was on, but there was no evidence of anyone in attendance. Action appeared to be centered in the kitchen—I'd come around to the back by then—where a card game and considerable beer consumption were taking place. Many longnecks had given their all. Bottles of bourbon and Scotch. One guy in a designer suit, two others in department-store distant cousins.

Newly awakened from its slumber in Glad bag and hand towel, the .38 Police Special felt strangely familiar to my hand.

One of the cheap-suit players was raking in chips as I came through the door. Undistracted, his counterpart pushed to his feet, gun halfway out as I shot. He fell back into his chair, which went over, as though its rear legs were a hinge, onto the floor. I'd tried for a shoulder, but it had been a while, and I hit further in on his chest. There was more blood than I'd have liked, too, but he'd be okay.

Thinking it over for a half-minute or so, the second cheap suit held up both hands, removed his Glock with finger and thumb and laid it on the table, just another poker chip.

Dean Atkison in his designer suit looked at his flunky with histrionic disgust and took a pull off his drink.

"Who the hell are you?" he said.

I was supposed to be watching him at that point, of course—cheap suit's cue. He almost had the Glock in hand when I shot. His arm jerked, knocking the Glock to the floor, then went limp. He stood looking down at the arm that would no longer do what he willed it to do. His fingers kept on scrabbling, the way cat paws will when the cat's asleep and dreaming of prey.

It was all coming back.

Atkison's eyes went from his fallen soldiers to me.

"Be okay if I call for help for my boys here?"

"Go ahead."

I stood by as he punched 911 into a cell phone, asked for paramedics, gave his address, and threatened the dispatcher. Thing about cell phones is you can't slam the receiver down.

"Think we might attend to business now?"

"We don't have any business."

I whacked his knee with the gun, feeling skin tear

and hearing something crunch. Blood welled through the expensive fabric. None of that should have happened.

"I live in a small town far away from here," I said. "Not far enough, apparently. A few days ago you brought your garbage to it."

He'd grabbed a hand towel off the table, was wrapping it around his knee.

"Paid some goddamn arrogant surgeon nine thousand to have that thing fixed, not six weeks ago. Now look at it."

"A man named Judd Kurtz came through. He didn't get through fast enough and wound up in jail. Then a couple of others came in his wake. None of them stayed."

"And I should care what happened in Bumfuck?"

I walked to him, helped wrap the towel.

"I need to know who Judd Kurtz is. I need to know if he's alive. And I need to know who the goons were who thought they could come into my town and tear it up."

"That's a lot of need."

Pulling hard at the ends of the towel, I knotted them.

"I was in a state prison for seven years," I told him. "I managed okay in there. There's not much I won't do."

He looked down at his shattered knee. Blood seeped steadily into the towel.

"Looks like a fucking Kotex," he said. "I'm a mess."
He shook his head. "I'm a mess—right?"

"It could be worse."

He pulled a napkin towards him. Started to reach under his coat and stopped himself. "I'm just getting a pen, okay?"

I nodded, and he took a bright yellow Mont Blanc out of his coat pocket, wrote, passed the napkin across. Classic penmanship, the kind you don't see anymore, all beautifully formed loops and curls—confounded by the absorbent napkin that blurred and feathered each fine, practiced stroke.

"My life's not all that much, mind you," he said, "but I'd like to know it doesn't end here."

I shook my head. Sirens of fire truck and ambulance were close by now.

Nodding towards the napkin, Atkison said, "You'll find what you need there."

What I needed right then was to go out the back door, and I did.

When first I held it, the gun had felt so familiar. The body has a memory all its own. I started the car, pulled the seat belt across and clicked it home. Slipped into gear. The body remembers where we've been even as the mind turns away. I eased off the clutch and pulled out, hot wires burning again within me, incandescent. Blinding.

Chapter Eight

My father's uniform hung in the back of a closet at the front of our house, in an unused bedroom. I found it there one rainy Saturday afternoon. It smelled of mothballs—camphor, as I'd later learn. Again and again I ran my fingers over its scratchy, stiff material. Dad never talked about his army time, what he'd done. In my child's mind I had him traversing deserts in Sherman tanks or diving fighter planes that looked much like Sopwith Camels through air thick with gunfire, smoke, and disintegrating aircraft. Much later, after his death, Mother told me he'd been a supply clerk.

I was, I don't know, twelve or so then. It was a couple of years after that that Al showed up in town.

He'd been in the service, people said, some place called Korea. Before, they added, he'd been the best fiddler in the county, but he'd given that up. He worked at the ice house, swinging fifty-pound blocks of ice off the ramp with huge tongs and all the time looking around, at the sky, at broken windows in the old power plant across the street, as though he wasn't really there, only his body was, doing these same things over and over, like a machine. He always had this half-smile on his face. He rented a room over the ice house but went there only to sleep. The rest of the time he was out walking the streets or sitting on the bench at the end of Main Street. He'd sit there looking off into the woods for hours. Pretty soon after I met him, when the ice house shut down, he lost his job. They let him stay on in the room, but then they tore the building down and he lost that too, so he lived out in the open, sleeping where he could. Later I'd get to know a lot of people like Al, people damaged deep inside, people whom life had abandoned but wouldn't quite let go of.

How did we meet? I honestly can't remember. I just remember everyone at school talking about him, then there's a skip, like on a record, and we're together throwing rocks into the Blue Hole, which everyone said had no bottom and half the world's catfish, or walking through Big Billy Simon's pasture with cows eyeing us, or sitting under a crabapple tree passing a Nehi back and forth.

It wasn't long before my folks heard about it and

told me to stay away from him. When I asked why, Mother said: He's just not right, son, that war did something to him.

But I went on seeing him, after school most every day. That was the first time I openly defied my parents, and things got tense for a while before they gave up. Many subsequent defiances took place in stone silence.

I was fourteen when Al and I met; a couple of years later I was getting ready to go off to college, first in New Orleans then in Chicago, little suspecting that but a few years down the line I'd be crawling through trees not unlike the ones Al stared into everyday. In the time I'd known him, I'd grown two feet taller and Al had aged twenty years.

I was sitting outside the tent one day taping up my boots when mail came around. I was on my third pair. In that climate, leather rotted fast. The French had tried to tell us, but as usual we didn't listen. They'd tried to tell us a lot of things. Anyway, it was five or six in the morning—you never could sleep much after that, what with all the bird chatter—and Bud chucked a beer my way, giving out the standard call, "Breakfast of champions," as I settled in to read my letter. Mom had written two pages about what was going on back home, who'd just married who, how so many of the stores downtown were boarded up these days, that the old Methodist church burned down. Newsreels from another world. Then there at the end she'd written: I'm sorry to have to tell you this, but Al died last week.

I grabbed another warm beer and went out to forest's edge, remembering that final summer.

For as long as I could remember, there'd been an old fiddle tucked away in the back of a closet no one used, in a cracked wood case shaped like a coffin. It had been my grandfather's, who played it along with banjo. I asked Dad if I could have it and after looking oddly at me, since I'd never shown much interest in music before, he shrugged and said he didn't see why not. This was late in his life, after the sawmill shut down, when he mostly just sat at the kitchen table all day.

I put some rubber bands around the case to hold it together and took it to Mr. Cohen, the school band director, who played violin in church some Sundays. Looked to him like a German-made fiddle from the 1800s, he said. He put on new strings and got the old bridge to stand up under them and gave me an extra bow he had. Not a full-size bow, only three-quarters, he said, but it'll do.

That afternoon I walked up to Al with the fiddle behind my back.

He eyed me suspiciously. "Whatchu got there, boy?"

I laid the case down on the bench and opened it. To this day I don't know what to call the expression that came over his face. I think maybe it's one of those things there's no word for.

"It's for you," I told him.

His eyes held mine for some time. He took the bow from under its clip. Al's hands always shook, but when he touched that bow they stopped. He weighed the bow in one hand, felt along its length, tightened the hair and bounced it against his palm, tightened it a little more.

Then he reached out with his left hand for the fiddle.

"It's all tuned up," I said.

He nodded, tucked the fiddle under his chin and sat there a moment with his eyes closed.

I don't remember what he played. Something I'd heard before, from my father or grandfather, one of the old fiddle tunes, "Sally Goodin" or "Blackberry Blossom," maybe. Next he tried a waltz.

He took the fiddle out from under his chin and held it against one leg, looking off at nothing in particular, smiling that half-present smile of his.

"It's just an old, cheap instrument," I said.

"No. The fiddle's fine," he said, putting it back in the case, clipping in the bow, carefully fastening the hooks. His hands were shaking again. "The music's in there. It just ain't in me no more."

We sat a while, hearing cars and trucks pass behind

us, looking out into the trees. Towards sundown when I was getting ready to head home, he said, "Reckon we won't be seeing much of each other for a time."

I nodded, too desperately young—soon enough, that would change—to understand good-byes.

After a moment he added: "Appreciate what you did, boy."

I picked up the case. I'd put on a new coat of paint, shiny black. In lowering light it looked like a puddle of ink, a pool of darkness. "Sure you don't want this?"

He shook his head. "Didn't mean about the fiddle, but I appreciate that too." Holding out his hand, he said, "Like you to have something. Got this when I was overseas, what they call in country, and it's been with me ever since. Want you should take it with you. Be your good luck charm."

A tiny cat carved out of sandalwood.

Chapter Nine

Dawn beat its proud pink breast as I and Chariot chugged to a stop. International news on the radio, a couple of ads for car dealers, now suddenly Jeremiah was a bullfrog, joy to the world.

Another mansion on the hill. Two cars, Mercedes, Lincoln, in a garage remarkably free of clutter. Ancient weeping willow like a bad sixties haircut outside, smell of fresh-brewed coffee from within. Older man in a terrycloth robe sitting at a table just inside glass doors from the patio. Wineglass of orange juice, possibly a mimosa, before him. Basket of bread, bowl of fruit. Scatter of woven rugs on what looked to be Saltillo tile and spotless. Mexican furniture in the room beyond. Lawn sprinklers went off behind me as I peered in.

Snooping about, I found a breachable window in the utility room and took advantage. Stood just inside listening, then slipped the door and listened some more before stepping through. No footsteps or other sounds of movement. Soft ersatz jazz from a radio out in the room by the patio.

He was tearing the horn from a croissant as I came up behind him and put thumbs to his neck.

"Compress carotids," I said, "and you shut off blood supply to the brain." I told him what I wanted to know. "We can talk when you come back around," I added, adding pressure as well, as his hands fell onto his lap and the others entered the room like silk. One of them facing me, the other one, the one that mattered, behind. Where they were before, I've no idea. I would have sworn he was alone.

Catching a glance from the one in front, I managed a half turn before the one behind closed on me and I joined the older man in darkness.

I came awake with a woman's face above me. The guy who had been standing behind me was male, no doubt about it. Not much doubt, either, that I was on the floor. Turning my head to the right, I saw swollen pink feet rising towards bare legs topped with a hem of ter-rycloth robe that in my confused state put me in mind of Elizabethan ruffled collars. Turned my head to the left and saw a body desperately attempting to drag itself out of harm's way, though at this point most of the harm it was likely to withstand had already befallen it.

"You're okay," the woman above me said. Not a question. Shortish dark hair pulled back. Hazel eyes in which glints of green surfaced and sank. She sounded pretty certain. I'd have to take her word for it.

"Mr. Aleché has agreed to call off his dogs. That right, Mr. Aleché?"

From high above terrycloth and tabletop, out of the clear blue sky up there, came a "Yes."

"One of his dogs seems to have taken bad," I said, glancing left again.

"Other one's a bit the worse for wear, too."

"Terrible shame."

Her face broke into a smile. Before, I'd always believed that to be merely a figure of speech.

"And lest you wonder, Mr. Aleché says these are the two men you're looking for. He seems to be under the impression that I know what's going on and that I am somehow your partner in this enterprise."

She held out her arm at a ninety-degree angle, inviting me to take it and lever myself to a sitting position. We grasped hands thumbs-over and, leaning hard into strong forearm and biceps, I pulled myself up.

"Mr. Aleché has also been kind enough to agree that by way of reparation he'll cover all medical expenses for your fellow officer and dispatcher. And he hopes you'll accept his apologies for his employees' misguided enthusiasm."

It's over, then, is what most people would think. But, even as she helped me up, I saw that she knew better, saw her clearly: the stance, feet planted squarely, center of gravity kept low, eyes taking it all in even as they appeared not to.

"You're a cop."

"That obvious, huh?" Again the smile. "I'm also your daughter." She held out a hand. "J. T. Burke."

Lots of scatlike noise and harrumphing from Sam Hamill back at the station, words to the effect that here was another fine mess I'd gotten him and MPD into, one shouldn't lie down with dogs, and it would be best if I were out of town by sundown.

"No sign of Judd Kurtz, huh?" Tracy Caulding asked. She'd stayed behind for her own counsel once Sam was done with me, then followed me out to the parking lot.

"Doubt there will be. Hope it didn't go too bad for you in there."

"About as you'd expect. What the hell was I thinking, tuck in the corners, it better not come back to bite his butt. Then he said, 'You need any help with this—stitches show up in the works, anyone whosoever tries giving you grief—You call me, you hear?'"

"Don't guess he added he'd be happy to have me

back on the job any time?"

"I don't believe that came up. Take care, Turner."

We surrendered J. T.'s rental Buick at a drop-off on Lamar, grabbing coffee to go at a Greek diner next door. The cups were shaped like Shriner's hats and, inexplicably, had rabbits on them. Not cuddly little bunnies, but huge kangaroo-thighed jackrabbits.

"Obviously they think a lot of you back at the station house," J. T. said as we pulled into traffic.

"I'm a legend here on the frontier."

"Must be nice." She stared silently out the window. "It all starts looking the same after a while, doesn't it? Same streets, same victims, same impossible stories and apologies."

We passed a car with the hood up, driver leaning into it. As we came abreast, he hiked his middle over the rim and slid in further. It looked as though the car were swallowing him piecemeal.

"If that's what you're looking for, an apology, I don't have one."

"Good. I've had enough of those, plenty to last me. And I'm not looking for anything—well, I was looking for you. But I found you, didn't I? So now I'm not."

"And how, exactly, did that come about, the finding me?"

"I talked to some people in town, learned about the

cabin, and went out there. There was a woman sitting on the porch."

"Val."

"I'd figured just to look around, maybe wait till you showed up. But I introduced myself, told her who I was, and we got to talking. She told me what's been going on, and that you were up here. I was waiting to turn in at the motel when I saw the Jeep pulling out."

"So you followed. Keeping well back, from the look of it."

She shrugged. "Old habit. Check exits before you go in, try to figure what's going down before you step in it. Like that."

"Cop thinking."

"You know how it is. Kind of takes over after a while."

Later, after one last stop in the city, well out of it and coming abreast of a long line of tarpaper shacks bordered by a service station and a church whose white paint had long ago gone to glory, we'd pick up the conversation. J. T.'s head turned to read the sign that told us we were entering the town of Sweetwater.

"So this is the South."

"Part of it, anyway. Disappointed?"

"Not really, just trying to get the lay of the land. Disappointment requires expectations. Like people have these scripts running in their heads about how life is supposed to go?"

"And you don't?"

"Mostly, no."

"Just take things as they come."

"I try." After a moment she added: "Seems to have worked for you."

We rode on past Sweetwater, through Magnolia and Ricetown, into mile after mile of cotton and soybean fields, plumes of dust on far horizons where pickups and farm machinery stalked the land.

"How's your mom?"

"Speaking of expectations." She laughed. "Somewhere in Mexico, last I heard. One of those gringo artist enclaves. That was over a year ago."

"She's an artist now?"

"I think she applied for the Grande Dame position. I'm sure they needed one, whether they knew it or not. Actually, she's mellowed."

"Some of us do. Others just wear down… And your brother?"

An ancient, battered lime green Volkswagen bus with lace curtains in the windows came up behind. Pointing to the VW's bumper sticker, J. T. said, "Kind of like that."

GOD WAS MY CO-PILOT
BUT WE CRASHED IN THE MOUNTAINS
AND I HAD TO EAT HIM

When I looked at her, she said, "You don't know, do you?"

I shook my head.

"Don died last year. Had a little more fun than he planned one Saturday night, got deeper than he thought, and flew off forever on his magic carpet of crack." Her eyes came to mine. "I'm sorry, I don't mean to be crude. Or cruel."

"It's okay."

Problems had lay coiled up beside Don in the crib from the day of his birth. Even then he wore a tense, fretful frown, as though he knew bad things were coming, as though he knew he had to be constantly on guard—though it probably wouldn't help much. Everything was a challenge, even the simple routines of daily life, getting up, getting dressed, leaving the apartment, shopping, a succession of near-insurmountable Everests. When things were going well, he managed to kind of plod along. But things didn't go well very often, or for very long. Choosing between breakfast cereals paralyzed him. On the phone, back when he used to call, he'd talk for hours about all these plans he had, never manage to carry through on the first half-step of any of them.

"I thought you knew. I'm sorry."

"Don't be. It's not as though we couldn't see it coming. The surprising thing is that he held out as long as he did. Were the two of you close?"

"Not for a long time. I tried. I'd go over to wherever he was crashing and check on him, try to be sure he ate something, got some rest."

"But you can't…"

"No," she said. "You can't. Like you said: we wear down. Or wear out."

Chapter Ten

"I'm sorry, I don't remember you. Should I?" His eyes moved aimlessly about the room. Guards had told me he was almost completely blind now. When I spoke, the eyes would come momentarily to me. Then they'd move away again.

Because of the blindness, Lou Winter had been kept out of the general population. But they'd got to him a time or two anyway, as the wing-shaped scar splitting the side of his face attested. Cons totally lacking in conscience, people who'd slit throats over a supposed insult and murder a grandmother for busfare, can get themselves worked into a moral frenzy over child molesters.

I told him who I was.

"I'm sorry. I'm afraid I don't remember much these days." Guards also told me that he'd had a series of small strokes over the years. "Everyone says that may be a good thing. I don't know what they mean by that. But thank you for coming."

After a pause he added, "Is there something I can do for you?"

"I just stopped by to say hello."

For a moment then I sensed the effort, the force of will. If he could just get hold of it, could just concentrate hard enough... But his eyes moved away, the curtains stayed shut, the play was over.

"I brought you this."

His hand reached out and found by sound the box I pushed across the table.

"It's not much. Some of the peppermints and circus peanuts the guards say you like, toiletries, a few other things."

But he had found the totem, the tiny cat carved out of sandalwood that Al had given me all those years ago, and was not listening. He held it close to his face, smelled it, rubbed it against his cheek where the scar ran down. I told him what it was. That a friend gave it to me.

"And now you've given it to me?"

I nodded, then said yes.

"Thank you." He shifted the totem from hand to hand. "Were we friends, then? Are we, I mean?"

"Not really. But we've known one another a long time."

"I'm sorry… so sorry I don't, can't, remember."

He held up the totem. "It's beautiful, isn't it? Small and beautiful. I can tell."

"Do you need anything, Lou? Is there anything I can do for you?"

"Good of you, son. But no." For that moment I would have sworn he was looking directly at me, that he saw me. Then his eyes went away. He closed his hand over the sandalwood cat. "I'm pretty well set up here." He nodded. "Yessir. Pretty well set up."

J. T. asked no questions when I got back to the car. But for some reason as we drove out of Memphis I started telling her about Lou Winter, about my first months on the force, about how hard it had been, going through those prison gates and doors. We sat together quietly then for a while until, looking out at the sign welcoming us to Sweetwater and the tarpaper shacks beyond, she said, "So this is the South."

Getting in towards town, I pointed out the Church of the Ark, a local landmark. It had once been just another First Baptist Church, but in 1921 during a major flood that wiped out most of the area, the building had miraculously lifted off its moorings and floated free, pastor and family taking aboard other survivors clinging to trees and housetops. It was renamed shortly thereafter.

Chapter Eleven

She'd grown up wherever her mother lit in her never-ending pursuit of best job, best house, best climate, best schools, best place to live. Took the name of her first stepfather, then resolutely refused to change it when others came along. That was the Burke. Just after she turned twenty-one she started calling herself J. T. Never felt like a Sandra, she said. It didn't stand for anything, "Just your initials."

She'd graduated high school at seventeen, done two years of prelaw in Iowa City, where Stepfather of the Month, a teacher of religion, had moved to study the Amish, then when that household broke up (and the marriage shortly thereafter—"in a roadside diner on the way to their new home's the way I always imagine it, him hugging his Bible as Mom steps out to flag a ride with some trucker"), she stayed behind, crashing with friends, hanging out in college bars. Got all that essential youth experience behind me in record time, she said, couple, three months, and was done with it. Never could get the knack of small talk, parties, hobbies, that kind of thing.

She'd driven to Chicago with a friend one weekend and stayed behind when the friend headed back. Worked as a corrections officer, which led to process serving, which led to a stint as a federal marshal. Now she worked up in Seattle, detective first grade. Knew she'd hit it right the first day on the job, went home glowing.

Then she hit the second day.

A sixteen-year-old had come in late one night and quietly murdered his whole family. Drowned his baby sister in the kitchen sink so she wouldn't have to see the rest, then with a Spiderman pillow smothered the six-year-old brother with whom he shared a room. Got the father's ancient service revolver from a box in the garage, loaded it with three bullets he'd bought on the schoolyard (just chance that they proved the right caliber) and shot both parents to death in their bed. Before shooting himself, he sat down at their bedside and painstakingly wrote out in block letters, vaguely Gothic, a note, just one word: ENOUGH.

But it wasn't, because the boy survived. Brian was his name. The round had gone through the roof of his mouth, wiping out any higher brain functions but leaving the brain stem untouched. He was still breathing, after all these years. And his heart went on beating. And one could only hope that his mind truly was gone, that he wasn't trapped in place somewhere in there going through all this again and again.

J. T. and her new partner, who had about two weeks more experience than she, were first call, right after patrol responded. Nothing can prepare you for a sight like that, she said. Or for what happens afterwards. It gets in your head like some kind of parasite and won't turn loose, it just keeps biting you, feeding on you.

She was quiet for a time then.

My partner quit the force not long after, she said. Why did I stick with it? Why do any of us?

So I told her a few stories of my own.

Chapter Twelve

Worst thing I've ever seen?

Not something I brought home from jungles halfway across the world. Not a body dead ten days of a long hot summer, not a black man hanging from the streetlamp of a strip mall in the New South. Or a gentle old blind man waiting to be strapped to a table in the name of justice and injected with poisons that will stop his lungs and heart.

I got the call one Friday night a year or so back, 11 p.m. or so. We'd had three or four quiet days, just the way we liked them. Traffic accident out on the highway, troopers would meet me there. I chalked code and destination on the board on my way out.

Four teenagers had taken a Buick for a joyride. Doug Glazer, the high-school principal's son; his girlfriend Jennie; local bad boy Dan Taylor; and multi-pierced Patricia Pope. They'd left a high school football game and seen the Buick there, keys in the slot, motor running. Why not. Drove it through town a couple of times, then out onto the interstate where they ran up under a semi at eighty-plus mph. I seen them comin', the driver said, I just couldn't get out of their way fast enough, I just couldn't get out of the way, not fast enough.

Most of Jennie's head was on the dashboard, mouth still smiling, lipstick bright. Dan Taylor and Pat Pope were a jumble of blood and body parts out of which one silver-studded ear protruded to catch light from the patrol car's bubble light. Glazer, the driver, had been thrown clear, not a mark on him. He looked quite peaceful.

We never know, do we? The hammer's hanging there as we go on about all the small things we do, paying bills, scouring sinks, restringing banjos, neglecting yet again to tell the one beside us how much he or she is loved.

Troopers had beat me to the site. The younger of them was throwing up at roadside. The senior one approached me.

"You'd be the sheriff."

"Deputy." We exchanged names, shook hands.

"Just a bunch of kids. Don't make any sense at all... Yo, Roy! you done over there?" Then to me: "Boy's first week on the job."

Since it was the interstate, they'd do the paperwork. I'd be left to notify the families.

"Gonna be a long hard night," Trooper Stanton said.

"Looks like."

"That yours?" he said, nodding towards the fire truck that had just pulled up. Benny waved from within. All we had was a volunteer department. Benny in real life worked at the auto parts store just down from city hall. He'd been through EMT training up at the capital.

"Sure is."

Took us better than two hours to clear the scene. Almost 3 a.m. when I knocked on Principal Glazer's door. I was there just under a half hour, then passed on to Jennie's parents, to Dan Taylor's father, Pat Pope's mother.

Sheila Pope lived in a trailer park outside town. She came to the screen door in a threadbare chenille robe, wearing one of those mesh sleep bonnets. It was pink. When I told her, there was no response, no reaction.

"You do understand—right, Mrs. Pope? Patricia's dead."

"Well… She was never a good girl, you know. I think I'll miss her, though."

That night I got back to the office not long before Don Lee showed up to take day shift. I made coffee, filled him in on the MVA, and headed home. In the rearview mirror I saw June pull into the spot I left.

A lazy, roiling fog lay on the water as I came around it to the cabin. One of the sisal-bound kitchen chairs on the porch had finally come apart. I suspected that the possum sitting close by may have had something to do with that. Maybe as a trained officer I should check for traces of twine in its teeth. I went in, poured milk into a bowl, and set it out on the porch.

She was never a good girl, you know. I think I'll miss her, though.

That's what a life came to.

Years ago, back when I had such arrogance as to think I could help anyone, I had as a patient a young woman who'd been raped and severely beaten while jogging. It happened near a reservoir. Every time she lifted a glass of water to drink, she said, it was there again. Of the attack she remembered nothing at all. What she remembered was being in ER just after, hearing caretakers above her talking about brain damage, saying: She'll only come back so far. I'd help her up from the chair at session's end. A well-mannered young man, her fiance Terry, always waited for her in the outer room.

Restless, turning as on a spit, I sensed a shadow fall across me and opened my eyes to see a possum crouched in the window. Possums are wild, they are resolutely not pets. But this one wanted in. I opened the window. The possum came in, sniffed its way down the bed, eventually fell asleep beside me. Not long after, I fell asleep myself.

I think I'll miss her, though.

Chapter Thirteen

Outside, inches away, a face leaned in close to the plateglass. Soon it loomed above our table.

"Trooper Rob Olson," he said without preamble. "We spoke earlier."

"Right."

"Okay if I turn the town over to you? Sheriff's been pulling more weight than he should, I don't really want to buzz him on this. When I signed on, I never counted on clocking this much time. Now the wife's threatening to change the locks."

Trooper Olson slid something across the table.

"What's this?"

"The beeper."

"We have a beeper now?"

"*You* do, anyway," J. T. said.

"Wear it in good health," Trooper Olson said.

By this time we were sitting in Jay's Diner over scrambled eggs, sliced tomatoes, and toast, complete with the little rack of bottled vinegar and oil, ketchup, steak sauce, and pepper sauce. Neither of us had been in the mood for dinner-type food.

"More coffee?" Thelma asked. Near as I could tell, she was here any time the diner was open. Hard to imagine what the rest of her life might be like. Which was odd, the fact that I didn't know, given what I knew about so many other lives hereabouts.

Both sides of the booth, we nodded.

"So you're on vacation."

"Only because they made me take it."

"And with nothing better to do, you figured What the hell, I'll track down the old man."

"Like I say, never got the knack of normal pastimes. I'd been thinking for some time about looking you up. Wasn't sure how you'd feel about that."

Nor was I.

"No one back there?"

"A guy, you mean?"

"Anyone."

"Not really. Handful of friends, mostly from the job." She glanced up to watch a new arrival, eyes following him from door to booth. Not from around here, you could tell that from the way he looked, way he moved. She saw it too. "I'm good at what I do, very good. I put most of myself into the work. Until recently that seemed enough."

"And now it's not?"

"I don't know. And most of all I hate not knowing."

"Maybe you just inherited a little of your mother's restlessness."

"Or yours."

Come home to roost, as they say around here. Probably didn't bear too much thinking, what other prodigal chickens might have shown up, for J. T. or for her brother Donald.

I set my cup down and waved off Thelma's query, via raised eyebrows, as to another refill.

"I have to thank you for what happened back there, J. T. But I also have to ask why you're here."

There was this strange energy to her, this sense of contained intensity in everything she did. It was in her eyes now, in the way she canted forward in the booth.

"I wanted to meet my father," she said. "It really is that simple. I think."

"Fair enough. How much vacation's left?"

"I'm still in the first week."

"Any plans?"

She shook pepper sauce onto her last piece of toast and made it disappear. Good eater.

"Tell the truth, I've started thinking maybe I could hang out here. With you. If you don't mind."

"I think I might like that."

"Done, then." She reached across to spear my last piece of tomato with her fork.

J. T. was half asleep as we drove to the cabin. When we came to the lake, she opened her eyes and looked out the window, at the water shimmering with light. "It's like the moon's come down to live with us," she said. Despite protests I got her settled in, insisting she take the bedroom, and to the sound of her regular breathing called Val. I hadn't had a phone at first or wanted one. Working with Don Lee pretty much demanded it, though. So I had one now. And I had a pet, Miss Emily the possum, gender no longer in doubt since she'd recently given birth to four tiny naked Miss Emilies living in a shoebox near the kitchen stove.

And I had a daughter.

"Apologies for calling so late," I said when Val answered. "Keep on the Sunny Side" by the Carter Family in the background.

"Any apologies you might conceivably owe me would be for *not* calling. How'd it go up there?"

I told her everything.

"Wow. You really cowboyed it."

"You okay with that, counselor?"

"As long as no warrants followed you home. Hope you didn't mind my telling J. T. where you were staying. She's there with you?"

"Asleep."

Strains of "The Ballad of Amelia Earhart" behind. *There's a beautiful, beautiful field, far away in a land that is fair.*

"So… Suddenly you have a family. Just like Miss Emily."

"I've had a family for a while now."

"Kind of."

"How's work been going?"

"Let's see. Yesterday the judge sent home a preteen whose older sister, eight years out of the house, submitted a deposition alleging long-term sexual abuse from the father. Fourteen-year-old firesetter Bobby Boyd's gone up to the state juvenile facility, where he'll be flavor of the month and learn a whole new set of survival skills."

"Business as usual."

"Always."

"Still, you stay in there batting."

"Never a home run. But sometimes we get a walk."

I stood listening to Val's breath on the line. From the kitchen came a squeal. One of the kids as Miss Emily rolled onto it? Or Miss Emily herself, one of them having bitten down too hard on a teat?

"When am I going to see you?" Val asked.

"What do you have on for tomorrow?"

"Tomorrow's Wednesday, always heavy. Three, maybe four court dates, have to meet with a couple of troopers at the barracks on upcomings."

"Any chance you could break away for dinner up this way?"

"I'd be late."

"We could meet you somewhere—that be better?"

"We, huh? I like that. No, I'll manage. Look for me by seven, a little after."

Moments passed.

"Racking my brain here," I said, "but I can't recall the Carter Family's ever having banjo on their recordings."

"You caught me. I've got you on the speaker—"

"Hence that marvelous fifties echo-chamber sound."

"—and I'm playing along with Sara, Maybelle, and A.P. Some days this is the only thing that relaxes me. Going back to a simpler time."

"Simpler only because we had no idea what was going on. Not even in our own country. Certainly nowhere else. We just didn't know."

"Whereas now we know too much."

"We do. And it can paralyze us, but it doesn't have to." Silence and breath braided on the line. "See you tomorrow, then?"

"Sevenish, right… Did you really say *hence?"*

"I admit to it. Makes up for your *whereas.*"

She left the line open. I heard the stroke, brush, and syncopated fifth string of her mountain-style banjo, heard the Carters asserting that the storm and its fury broke today.

Chapter Fourteen

We were sitting to dinner the next night when the beeper went off and I went Shit! I'd forgotten I had the thing. Dropped it on the little table inside the door when I got home the night before and hadn't thought of it since. There it sat as I'd gone in to pull the day shift. There it still sat.

One of Miss Emily's babies was doing poorly when I got home. Seemed to be having difficulty breathing, muscle tone not good, floppy head, dark muzzle. Miss Emily kept carrying it away from the shoebox and leaving it on the floor. I'd pick it up and put it back, she'd carry it off again. Val came in and immediately scooped it up, rummaged through the medicine cabinet until she found an old eyedropper, cleaned out its mouth and throat, blew gently into its nose. Then she put it in her shirt pocket "to warm." When she pulled it out a half hour later, it looked ready to take over the shoebox and take on all comers.

"What *can't* you do?" I asked her.

"Hmmm. Well, world peace for one. And I'm still working on bringing justice to the Justice Department." She smiled. "Possums are easy. They're what I had for pets when I was growing up. You named these guys yet?"

It hadn't even occurred to me.

"Okay, then. That's Lonnie, that one's Bo, that one's Sam."

"The Chatmons."

"You have any idea how few people there are alive on this earth who would know that?"

"And the fourth one, odd man out, has to be Walter Vinson."

"Right again."

Wearing one of my T-shirts, J. T. emerged from the back room. "There's the problem with all you old folks," she said, "forever going on about the great used-to-be."

"Old folks, huh?" Val said.

"Well, you have to admit he weighs down the demographics." The two of them hugged. "Good to see you again."

"Me too. Glad you found him—and in the nick of time, from what he tells me."

"Pure chance. Seems I'm always blundering into things without knowing what's going on."

"May be a family trait."

J. T. laughed. "We were just talking about that… Came out all right in the end, anyway."

We'd assembled, quite naturally, in the kitchen, where Miss Emily watched us warily from her shoebox. Southerners are known to dine sumptuously on possum.

I pulled a dish of cornbread out of the oven, along with a casserole of grits, cheese, and sausage. Turned the fire off under a pot of greens after dropping in a dollop of bacon fat. Miss Emily and her brood were safe, for the moment.

"This food looks, I don't know," J. T. said, "weird?"

Val took the challenge. "This? This is nothing! Wait till he does the pig tails for you, or squirrels fried whole, with hollow eye sockets staring up at you."

"Maybe I'll just have a beer."

But after a while her fork found its way into the mound of grits on her plate, then into the greens, just reconnoitering mind you. Next thing you know, she's at the stove spooning up seconds.

"Must be in my blood," she said as she rejoined us. "Strange to be eating this time of night, like a normal person. Normal except for the food, I mean." She had a forkful or two before going on. "I usually work nights. Prefer them, really. The department has rotating shifts, like most, but I always swap when I can. The city's different at night. *You're* different."

"Plus most of chain-of-command is home asleep."

"There's that too. You're really *out there.*"

On the edge, yes. "And night's when the cockroaches come out." It was an old homily among lawmen, probably been around since the praetorian guards. Hail Caesar, they say behind their lanterns. And here come the cockroaches.

"Right. So, like them, that's when I usually eat. Great steaming mounds of indigestible food at two in the morning. Rib-eye steaks like shoe soles, potatoes with chemical gravy, caramelized burgers, vulcanized eggs."

"Food that sticks to your ribs," Val said, invoking a homily every bit as ancient.

"Nothing like *this,* of course."

My daughter had kept her sense of humor. Kind of work we do, what we see day after day, so many don't. Never trust a man (or woman) without a sense of humor. That's the first rule. The *other* first rule, of course, is never trust anyone who tells you who to trust.

"Rest of the night and day's mostly coffee," J. T. went on, maybe a bowl of oatmeal once the paperwork's done. Then home to movies I picked out over the weekend and, two to four hours later, sleep, if I'm lucky. By three in the afternoon, mind that I've got home at like nine, ten in the morning, I'm up again and marking time. Put a pot of coffee on and drink the whole thing while watching *Cops*, *Judge Judy*, and the rest. Still have Mother's old Corningware percolator and use it every day."

"Blue flowers on the side?"

"That's the one."

"And it still turns out drinkable coffee?"

"Following a few rounds of bleach and baking soda, yeah—it was in storage a long time."

That's when the beeper went off.

Most phone service these days is automated, but in small towns like ours, operators are still in the thick of it. They dial for the elderly or disadvantaged, do directory work, take emergency calls.

The number from the beeper was answered on the first ring.

"Sorry to disturb you, Deputy."

"That you, Mabel? It's what? eleven o'clock at night? You don't ever get off?"

"We don't have anyone on the switchboard after six, no money for it, they say. So emergency calls get routed to my home phone. I tried the office first, just in case. No one there."

There wouldn't be. With my return, the retired boys

from the barracks had flown. Lonnie and I were doing broken runs down the field of days, passing the ball back and forth.

"It's Miss June. Called in saying there was trouble out to her place."

"I thought she was living with her parents."

"Nope. Moved into a little house out on Oriole, belonged to Steve and Dolly Warwick when they were alive. Now it's rented out by their son."

"What kind of trouble are we talking, Mabel?"

"Break-in, I'd say, from the sound of it."

"Why didn't June call her father? He's still the sheriff."

"Can't say. They've had problems in the past—everyone knows that. But she specifically asked for you."

I took down the address such as it was, offered apologies to Val and J. T., Miss Emily and her progeny. I reminded J. T. that, if a strange man showed up at the door, one who looked like he belonged here, then it was probably just my neighbor Nathan.

"You mean like one of the trees trying to fake its way inside?"

"He won't come inside, but yeah, that's Nathan."

June was sitting on the porch, bare feet hanging over and almost touching ground, as I pulled in. House was built in the thirties. Floods being a regular part of life back then, houses were built high.

I climbed down from the Chariot but didn't advance, eyes from old habit sweeping windows, porch, and nearby trees, looking for anything that didn't fit.

"You okay, June?"

"Fine." She dropped the few inches to the ground and stood. "Thanks for coming."

"You're welcome."

"Permission to come aboard."

"What?"

"That's what they're always saying in old movies, old books. Permission to come aboard."

As I started towards her she turned, went up the steps through the door and into the house. I found her just inside, surveying the wreckage. Every drawer had been pulled and upended, cushions sliced into, chairs and tables and shelves broken apart, lamps and appliances overturned.

"Funny thing about violation," she said. "Once it happens, somehow you expect it to keep on happening, you know? Like that's how the world's going to work from now on." She turned to me. "Of course you know. Would you like a drink? I keep a bottle of Scotch here for Dad."

I said sure, and she went off to the kitchen to get it.

"Mind if we go back outside?"

Nothing had changed out there. I sat beside her at the edge of the porch.

"When you were injured," I said after a while. "You were carrying a handgun."

"And you never asked why."

"Not till now."

Before, I'd never seen much of Lonnie in her. Now, as she ducked her head and looked off into the distance, I did.

"I had a teacher back in twelfth grade. Mr. Sacher. He'd lost both arms in the Korean war. He'd pick up the textbook between the heels of the hands of stiff prosthetic arms and place it gently on the desk. We're all good at one thing, he told us over and over. The problem lies in finding out what that one thing is.

"Mr. Sacher's thing was comedy. He'd get a bunch of us in the car and, eyes rolling in mock terror, throw up his hands. But he'd be steering with his knees on the wheel. He'd bring in a guitar and make terrible efforts to play it.

"Mr. Sacher may have been right. The one thing I seem to be good at is picking bad men."

"This," I said, remembering the black eye she had tried to conceal, "wouldn't be the work of the guy you were with a year or so back, would it?"

"No way. But there've been others."

"Any of them likely to have done this?"

"I don't think so."

"So maybe it was random."

We sat silently.

"Maybe you should give some thought to coming back to work."

"I don't…" I saw the change in her eyes. "You're right. Give me tomorrow to clean up this mess. I'll be in the day after. Do me good to have something else to concentrate on."

"Great." Finishing my Scotch, I set the glass on the warped boards of the porch. Those boards looked as old and as untamed as the trees about us. "Mabel said you asked for me."

"I did."

"How do you want to handle this?"

"There's not much to handle, is there?"

"There's Lonnie."

She nodded. "I thought you could talk to him, tell him what happened. I go to him with this, it'll be my fault. The losers I hang out with. When am I going to learn. My misspent life."

"I'll talk to him, first thing in the morning."

"I appreciate it."

"Be good to have you back, June."

J. T. was sitting out on the porch when I got home. I settled beside her. Frogs called to one another down in the cypress grove.

"Val gone?"

"Hour or so back."

"Feel up to helping a friend clean house?" I asked.

Chapter Fifteen

Back when I worked as a therapist, having acquired something of a reputation around Memphis, I tended to get the hard cases, the ones no one else wanted. Referrals, they're called, like what Ambrose Bierce said about good advice—best thing you can do is give it to someone else, quick. And for the most part these referrals proved a surly, deeply damaged lot, none of them with much skill at or inclination towards communication, all of them leaning hard into the adaptive mechanisms that had kept them going for so long but that were now, often in rather spectacular fashion, breaking down.

I was therefore somewhat surprised at Stan Bellison's calm demeanor. I knew little of him. He was, or had been, a prison guard, and had suffered severe job-related trauma. The appointment came from the state authority.

Why are you here? is the usual, hoary first question, but this time I needn't ask it. Stan entered, sat in the chair across from me, and, after introducing himself, said: "I'm here because I was held hostage."

Two inmates had, during workshop, dislodged a saw blade from its housing and, holding it against one guard's throat, taken another—Stan, who tried to come to his fellow guard's aid—hostage. Sending everyone else away, the inmates had blockaded themselves in the workshop and, when contacted, announced they would only speak to the governor. The first guard they released as a gesture of goodwill. Stan, whom they referred to as Mr. Good Boy, they kept.

"You were a cop," Bellison said. Once again I remarked his ease.

"Not a very good one, I'm afraid."

"Then let's hope you're better as a therapist," he said, and laughed. "I don't want to be here, you know."

"Few do."

His eyes, meeting mine, were clear and steady.

Each day the inmates cut off a finger. The crisis went on eight days.

On the last, the lead inmate, one Billy Basil, stepped through the door to pick up a pizza left just outside, only to meet a sniper's bullet. The governor hadn't come down from the capitol to parlay, but he had sent instructions.

"So then it was over, at least," I said. "The trauma, what they did to you, that'll be with you for a long time, of course."

"You don't understand," Stan Bellison told me. "The other inmate? His name was Kyle Beck. That last day, as he stood staring at Billy's body in the open door, I came up behind him and gouged out his eyes with my thumbs."

He held up his hands. I saw the ragged stumps of what had been fingers. And the thumbs that remained.

Chapter Sixteen

"She'll never learn, will she?"

"That's what she said you'd say."

We were sitting on the bench outside Manny's Dollar \$tore, where almost exactly a year ago Sarah Hazelwood and I had sat, when her brother was murdered. Lonnie took a sip of coffee. A car passed down Main Street. Another car. A truck. He sipped again. A light breeze stirred, nosing plastic bags, leaves, and food wrappers against our feet. "You still have that possum you told me about?"

"Miss Emily. Yeah. Got a family now. Ugliest little things you can imagine."

Brett Davis came out of the store buttoning a new flannel shirt, deeply creased from being folded, over the one he already wore.

"Lonnie. Mr. Turner."

"First purchase of the millennium, Brett?"

"Last one just plumb fell apart when Betty washed it. Says to me, Brett, you better come on out here, and she's holding up a tangle of wet rags. Damn shame."

"For sure." Lonnie touched forefinger to forehead by way of saying good-bye. Brett climbed into his truck that always looked to me like something that had been smashed flat and pumped back out, maybe with powerful magnets.

"June's right," Lonnie said after a while. "I've always blamed her, always turned things around in my mind so that they got to be her fault. I don't know why."

"Disappointment, maybe. You expect as much from her as you do from yourself—and expect much the same things. We construct these scenarios in our minds, how we want the world to be, then we kick at the traces when the world's not like that. We're all different, Lonnie. Different strengths, different weaknesses."

"Don't know as I ever told you this before, but there's times I feel flat-out stupid around you. We talk, and you tell me what I already know. Which has got to be the worst kind of stupid."

"It's all the training I've had."

"The hell it is."

Lonnie took June to dinner that night, just the two of them. She'd spent the day, with J. T.'s help, getting her house back in order. He put on his best shirt and a tie and the jacket of a leisure suit that had been hanging in the back of his closet for close on to thirty years and met her at her door with a spray of carnations and drove all the way over to Poplar Crossing, to the best steakhouse in the county. "Everybody must of thought this was just some poor foolish old man romancing a young woman," June said when she came in to work the next morning.

With her there to hold down the fort, I decided to go visit Don Lee. He'd been transferred to the county hospital an hour or so away.

He was off the respirator now. An oxygen cannula snaked across the bed to his nose. Water bubbled in the humidifier. IV bags, some bloated, others near collapse, hung from poles. One of the poles held a barometer-like gadget that did double duty, registering intercranial pressure and draining off fluid.

"He's intermittently conscious," a nurse told me, "about what we'd expect at this point. He's family? A friend?"

"My boss, actually." There was no reason to show her the badge but I did anyway. She said she was sorry, she'd be right outside the door catching up on her charting, and left us alone.

I put my hand against Don Lee's there on the bed. His eyes opened, staring up at the ceiling's blankness.

"Turner?"

"I'm here, Don Lee."

"This is hard."

"I know."

"No. This is *hard*."

I told him what went down in Memphis.

"Kind of let the beast out of the cage there, didn't you?"

"Guess I did, at that."

"You okay?"

"Yeah."

"Good. I'm tired, really tired… Why did someone stick an icepick in my head, Turner?"

"It's a monitor."

"Man-eater?"

"No, monitor."

"Big lizard you mean."

"Not really."

He seemed to be thinking that over.

"They keep telling me and I keep forgetting: June's okay, right?"

"She's fine. Back at work as of today."

I thought he'd fallen off again when he suddenly said, "You sure you don't want to be sheriff?"

"I'm sure."

"Smart move," he said.

★

I was backing the Chariot out of a visitor's space when the beeper went off. I sat looking at the number while a car and an SUV roughly the size of a tank blared horns at me.

June.

I pulled back into the space, earning a middle-finger salute from the tank driver, and went to use the phone in the hospital lobby.

"How's Don Lee?" June asked.

"Looking good. Still gonna be a while. So what's up?"

"Maybe nothing. Thelma called. From the diner? Said some guy was in there early this morning. Waiting in his car when they came in to open, actually. Just ordered coffee. Then a little later—she and Gillie and Jay were setting up, of course, but she swung by a time or two to check on him—he asked after you. Said he was an old friend."

Any old friends I was supposed to have, I probably didn't want to see.

"When Thelma said he should check in at the sheriff's office, he said well, he was just passing through, pressed for time. Maybe he'd come back."

"Thelma say what he looked like?"

"Slight, dark skin and hair, wearing a suit, that was dark too, over a yellow knit shirt buttoned all the way up. Good shoes. Thing was, Thelma said, he didn't ask the kind of questions you'd expect. Where you lived, what you did for a living, all that. What he wanted to know was did you have a family, who your friends were."

"Thanks, June. He still around?"

"Got back in his car, Thelma said—a dark blue Mustang, I have the license number for you—and drove off in the direction of the interstate."

"I'm on my way in. See you soon."

Half an hour later I pulled off the road onto the bluff just above Val's house. The old Ames place, as everyone still called it. Val was up at the state police barracks doing her job, of course, but a dark blue Mustang sat in her drive.

I went down through stands of oak and pecan trees trellised with honeysuckle, through ankle-deep tides of kudzu, to the back door opening onto the kitchen. No one locked doors here, and the kitchen would have no interest for him.

I also had the advantage of knowing the house and its wood floors. Focusing on creaks above, I followed his progress: master bedroom, hallway, second and third bedrooms, bath. Then the tiny tucked-wing room probably meant for servants, and the hallway again.

"You'd be Turner," he said from the top of the stairs.

One cool guy. Sure of himself and waiting to see which way the wind blew.

I put a round through one knee. He came tumbling down the stairs with left hand and drawn weapon bumping behind him, to the base, where my foot pinned his wrist.

"Apologies first," I said. "You're obviously not one of the thickneck boys. They wouldn't know subtlety if it ran over them, then backed up and had another go."

"Contract," he said.

"Who's paying?"

"You know how it works. I can't tell you that."

I moved the snout of the Police Special vaguely in his direction, a sweeping motion. "Ankle or knee?"

I used Val's phone to call and tell June I was going to be a little later than I'd thought. Then I drove back to the hospital, one of Val's sheets wrapped tight around my passenger's leg. There wasn't much vessel damage, but joints do get bloody. Ask any orthopedic surgeon.

I was doing just that ("Case like this, we can rebuild the joint from the fragments, adding a bit of plastic here and there—sometimes that's best, staying with the original—or we can replace the whole thing. The newest titanium appliances are remarkable") when Val walked through the double doors.

"June called me."

I thanked the doctor and said I'd get back to him about cost, responsibility, and so on.

"Not a problem," he said. "Mr. Millikin had proof of insurance with him. He's fully covered. Says he wants to be the man of steel. I've got to go finish a procedure up in OR—got interrupted to check him out. Then we'll have him brought up." Nodding his leave-taking: "Sheriff. Ma'am."

"What the hell is going on?" Val asked. "This guy was in my house? Why was this guy in my house? Who the hell is this guy?"

In the basement we found a place to get coffee, not really a cafeteria, more a kind of commissary, and I walked her through what had happened.

"So, what? He was going to hold me hostage?"

"Or worse. Beyond saying it's a contract, he won't talk."

"This ties in with what went down in Memphis."

I nodded.

"Going back in turn to Don Lee's arrest of what's-his-name—Judd Kurtz?"

"Right again."

"From what little I know about it, farming out enforcement work's not the way these people usually handle things."

"True enough. What I'm thinking is, given how it went down last time, they've elected for a low profile. Set it up so nothing can be traced back to them."

Blowing across her coffee cup—absolutely superfluous, since the coffee was at best lukewarm—Val tracked a young woman's progress down the line. An elaborate tattoo scored the nape of her neck. She wore studded boots and sniffed at everything she took from narrow, glass-shuttered shelves. Most of it, she set back.

"These guys have the longest memories of all," Val said. "They've got wars that have been going on for centuries. Sooner or later, they don't hear from their scout, they'll figure out it went wrong."

"We could send them his head."

Having reached the register, the tattooed young woman stood beaming at the cashier as he spoke, waited, and spoke again. Then the smile went away and she came back into motion.

"Just kidding," I said. "You're right. They'll wait a while, but they'll be back. Someone will."

Chapter Seventeen

That night around eleven I got a call. Mabel had routed it through to me at home. I could barely hear the speaker over the jukebox and roar of voices behind.

"This the sheriff?"

"Deputy."

"Good enough. Reckon you better get on out here."

"Where's here?"

"The Shack. State Road Forty-one, mile past the old cotton gin."

I told him I was on my way and hung up.

"Where's Eldon playing these days?" I asked Val.

"Place called The Shack. Why?"

"Thought so. They've got trouble."

"He okay?"

"I don't know. You be here when I get back?"

"I have a home day tomorrow, and some briefs I need to get started on tonight. Call me?"

I said I would, and asked her to leave a note for J.T. in case she woke while I was gone. Clipped the holster on my belt and headed for the Chariot.

The Shack was surprisingly well constructed, built of wood and recently repainted, dark green with lighter highlights. Shells paved the parking lot, crunching as I walked across. Specimens of every insect native to the county swarmed in dense clouds around the yellow lights at the door.

The bar took up the wall just inside and to the right, allowing the bartender to keep an eye on everything. The ceiling was low, bar lit by a single overhead light that filled the shelves with shadows.

The bandstand, little more than a pallet extending a foot or so above the floor, occupied the corner opposite the bar. Most of the patrons were gathered there. Upon hearing the heavy door, they looked around. How they heard it, I don't know, what with the war sounds coming from the jukebox.

"Turn that thing off."

The bartender reached under the bar. A saxophone solo died in mid-honk, like a shot goose.

The crowd drew back as I approached. Eldon sat on the edge of the bandstand. One eye was swollen almost shut; blood, black in the half-light, black like his face, blotched the front of his shirt. His guitar lay in pieces before him. The bass player stood backed against the wall, hugging his Fender. The drummer, still seated, twirled a stick in each hand.

"Come *on*, you son'va'bitch! Stand up and fight like a goddamn man!" This from a stocky guy with his back to me.

I put a hand gently on his shoulder and he came around swinging, then grunted as I tucked one fist in his armpit, grabbed his wrist with the other, pulled hard against the latter and leaned hard into the former. When he brought the other hand around to strike, I gave his wrist a twist. What must have been a buddy of his started towards me, saying "Hey man, you can't—" only to have a drumstick strike him squarely between the eyes. He staggered back. The drummer, who'd thrown the stick like a knife, wagged a finger in warning.

"You okay, Eldon?"

"Yeah."

"How about you?" I asked the stocky guy. "You cooled down?"

He nodded, and I let go, backing off. Watching his eyes. I saw it there first, then in the shift of his feet. Stamped hard on his instep, and when that knee buckled, I kicked the other foot out from under him.

"Don't get up till you're ready to behave." Then to

Eldon: "What's this all about?"

"Who knows? Guy starts hanging around the band-stand, has something to say every minute or two, I just smile and nod and ignore him. So he starts getting louder. Tries to get up onstage at one point and spills a beer on my amp. So then he stumbles getting down and starts yelling that I pushed him. Next thing I know, he's grabbed my guitar and smashed it."

"You want me to take him in?"

"Hell no, Turner. Not like I ain't been through this before. Just get his buddy there to take him the fuck home and let him sleep it off."

I helped the man up.

'Your lucky day," I told him. "Give me your bill-fold." I took the driver's license out. "You come pick this up tomorrow and we'll have a talk. Now get the hell out of here."

I waited at the bar while Eldon borrowed a towel from the bartender and went in the bathroom to clean up. He came back looking not much better.

"Shirt kinda makes me homesick for tie-dye. Buy you a drink?"

"Tomato juice."

"And a draft for me," I told the bartender.

The jukebox came back on. I looked hard at the bartender and the volume went down about half.

"He wanted you to fight him."

"Sure did."

"But you didn't."

Eldon looked off at the bandstand, where drummer and bassist were packing up.

"Must be about six, seven years ago now. Club down in Beaumont. I's out back on a break and this guy comes up talkin' 'bout. You shore can play that thing, boy. Gets up in my face like a gnat and won't go away."

He finished off his juice.

"I damn near killed him. Vowed that day I'd never take another drink and I'd never fight another man. You ever killed anyone, Turner?"

"Yeah. Yeah, I have."

"Then you know."

I nodded.

The bass player had scooped up what was left of Eldon's guitar and put it in the case. He brought the case over and set it at Eldon's feet.

"Talk to you tomorrow," Eldon said.

"Don't call too early." An old joke: they both grinned.

Out on the floor, four or five couples were boot-scooting to Merle Haggard's "Lonesome Fugitive."

"Back when I played R&B, I always had half a dozen or more electric guitars," Eldon said. "Have me a Gibson solid-body, a Gretsch, one of those Nationals shaped like a map, a Telecaster or a Strat. Ain't had but this old Guild Starfire for years now. When I bought it, place called Charlie's Guitars in Dallas, it had the finish torn off right above the pickup, where this bluesman had had his initials glued on. Guess he slapped it on his next guitar. And guess *I'll* be heading up to Memphis in the morning to do some shopping."

Val hadn't gone home after all. She lay on the couch with one bent leg balanced across the other forming a perfect figure 4. Miss Emily was asleep on the armrest by her head. I tucked a quilt around Val, then went out to the kitchen and poured myself a solid dose of bourbon.

I'd made pasta earlier, and the kitchen still smelled of garlic. The back door was open. A moth with a body the size of my thumb kept worrying at the screen door. Frogs and night birds called from the lake.

J.T. had all but fallen asleep at the dinner table. Used to being busy, she said. Not being wears me out, plus there's the shift thing. She insisted on cleaning up, then the minute it was done went off to bed. That the bed was hers was something *I'd* insisted on, despite voluble protests, when she came to stay with me. I'd taken the couch. And now the couch had been retaken, by Val. And Emily. The house was filling up fast.

"Is Eldon okay?"

Wrapped in the quilt, Val stood in the doorway. Miss Emily bustled around her to go check on the kids.

"A little the worse for wear—but aren't we all." I told her what had happened. "Thought you were going home."

She sat across from me, reached for my glass and helped herself to a healthy swallow.

"So did I. But the more I thought…"

I nodded. There are few things like home invasion to rearrange the furniture in your head. "Give it time."

She yawned. "That's it, enough of the good life. I'm going back to bed."

"To couch, you mean."

"There's room for both of us."

"There's barely room for you."

"So where will you sleep?"

"Hey, eleven years in prison, remember? I can sleep anywhere. I'll grab a blanket or two, take the floor in here."

"You sure?"

"Go to couch, Val."

"Don't stay up too long."

"I won't, but I'm still a little wired. I'll just sit here a while with Miss Emily and family."

"Night."

I poured another drink and sat wondering why Miss Emily had chosen to live among people, and what she thought about them. Hell, I wondered what I thought about them.

Satisfied the kids were all right, Miss Emily had climbed to the window above the sink, one of her favorite spots. Glancing up at her, I saw her head suddenly duck low, ears forward.

Then I saw the shadow crossing the yard.

I was out the door before I'd thought about it, taking care not to let the screen door bang. A bright moon hung above the trees. My eyes fell to their base, seeking movement, changes in texture, further shadows. Birds and frogs had stopped calling.

Never thought they'd show up this soon.

I eased across the porch and onto the top step, looking, listening. Stood like that for what seemed endless minutes before the floorboards creaked behind me. I turned and he was there, one sinewy arm held up to engage my own.

"Nathan!"

His grip on my wrist loosened.

"Someone been up in them woods," he said, "going on the better part of a month now."

"You know who?"

He shook his head. "But early on this evening, one of them came in a little too close to the cabin, then made the mistake of running. Dog took out after him, naturally, came back looking pleased with hisself. So I tracked him down this way. Blood made it some easy."

We found him minutes later by the lake, lying face-down. Early twenties, wearing cheap jeans and a short denim jacket over a black T-shirt, plastic western boots. Blood drained rather than pumped from his thigh when I turned him over.

Nathan shook his head.

Dogs hereabouts aren't pets, they're functional, workers, brought up to help provide food and protect territory. Nathan's had gone at the young man straight on, taking out an apple-sized chunk of upper thigh and, to all appearances, a divot from the femoral artery.

"Damn young fool," Nathan said. "Reckon we ought to call someone."

"No reason to hurry." I took my fingers away from the young man's carotid. When I did, something on his forearm caught light. I pushed back his sleeve. "What's that look like to you?"

Nathan bent over me.

"Numbers."

Chapter Eighteen

I remembered them from childhood. I was six years old. They were everywhere. Covering the trees, climbing the outside walls of the house and barbecue pit, swarming up telephone and electric poles, making their way along the chicken wire around dog runs. There they erupted from the back of their shells and unfurled wings. Hadn't been there at all the night before. Then suddenly thousands of them: black bodies the size of shrimp and maybe an inch long, transparent wings, red eyes. The males commenced to beat out tunes on their undersides, thrumming on hollow, drumlike bellies. As the sun warmed, they played louder and harder. Dogs, the wild cat that lived under the garage, chickens, mockingbirds, and bluejays ate their fill. People did too, some places, Dad told me.

People thereabouts still called them locusts. My

friend Billy and I collected their husks off trees and the house and lined them up in neat rows on the walls of our bedrooms. Later I'd learn their real name: cicadas. I'd learn that they emerge in thirteen- or seventeen-year cycles, coming out in May, all dead by June. The male dies not long after coupling, whereupon the female takes to a tree, cuts as many as fifty slits in one of the branches, and deposits 400 to 600 eggs. Once her egg supply is gone, she dies too. Six to eight weeks later the nymphs hatch and fall to the ground, burrowing in a foot or so and living off sap sucked from tree roots until it's their turn to emerge, climb, shed skins, unfurl wings.

Most of this I learned forty-odd years later.

Not a title—my name, Bishop Holden told me at our first meeting. He and I were of an age. When, after my childhood experience of them, the cicadas came again, I was in a jungle half a world away and Bishop was in line at the local draft where, told to turn his head and cough, he instead grabbed the doctor's head in both hands and planted a hard, wet kiss on his lips. He was carried away, discoursing incoherently of conspiracies and government-funded coups, and remanded by courts to the local psychiatric hospital. He'd been in and out of one or another of them most of his life. At the last, during convulsions caused by a bad drug reaction, he'd bitten off the finger of an orderly trying to help him and developed something of a taste for flesh. He'd bagged another finger, half an ear, and a big toe before (as he said) putting himself on a strict diet.

He had skin like a scrubbed red potato, pouchlike, leathery cheeks. In khakis, cardigan, and canvas shoes, he reminded me of Mr. Rogers.

"Ready for them?" he asked. Our chairs stood at a right angle, a small shellacked table pushed close in to the apex. I turned my head to him. His turned to the window.

Ready for what exactly, I asked.

"The cicadas. It's time. I've called them."

Called them up from the depths of the earth itself, he said; and while I was never to learn much about Bishop Holden, over the next hour and in later sessions (until one bright morning he bit through the chain of a charm bracelet on the wrist of a teenage girl passing his breakfast sandwich through a carryout window) I learned quite a lot about cicadas.

Now, so many years later and a bit further south, it was time for them again.

Two abandoned shells, spurs hooked into mesh, hung on the screen of the window above the sink when I got up the next morning. It sounded as though a fleet of miniature farm machinery, tiny tractors and combines and threshers, had invaded the yard.

Thanks to Bishop, I knew that three distinct species

always surface at the same time, and that each has not only its own specific sound but a favored time of day as well. Someone once said that the three sounded in turn like the word *pharaoh,* a sizzling skillet, and a rotary lawn sprinkler. The morning cicadas, the siz-zlers, were hard at their work.

"What the hell *is* that racket?" J. T. asked from the doorway. I told her.

She came up close behind me and stood watching as they swarmed.

"Jesus. This happen often?"

"Every seventeen years, like clockwork. No one understands why. Or how, for that matter."

I filled her in on cicadas as I pulled eggs and cheese from the icebox and poured coffee for a reasonable facsimile of Val that wandered in—what a writer might be tempted to call a working draft. I dropped a tablespoon of bacon grease from the canister on the stove into a skillet, laid out bread in the toaster oven I really needed to remember to clean. Dump the crumbs, at least.

"Did I hear cars?" Val asked as I poured her second cup. The rewrite was coming along nicely.

"Doc Bly and his boy."

"Not a delivery, I assume." Doc ran the mortuary. He was also coroner.

Putting breakfast on the table, I told them about the

young man who'd died out by the lake.

"He'd been living in the woods?"

"According to Nathan. More than one of them."

"Have any idea what's with the numbers?"

"Not really."

"They were permanent?"

"Looked to be."

"Not just inked in, like kids used to do back in school?"

"Not that crude. Not professional, either, but carefully done. In prison there were guys who'd do tattoos for cigarette money. They used the end of a guitar string and indelible ink, took their time. Some of them got damned good at it. That's what this reminded me of, that level of skill."

"Nathan have any idea what these people are doing up there?"

"None."

"But now you're going to have to find out."

"Guess I am."

"I'll come along," J. T. said.

Half an hour later we were scraping cicadas off the Chariot's windshield as Val pulled out on her way to work. J. T. went in to get the thermos of coffee we'd forgotten and came back out saying the beeper had gone off while she was inside.

"On the table," she said.

Of course it was.

And of course it was the bugs. Raising hell everywhere, June told me, getting in houses that left their
windows open, in water troughs and switch boxes and
attics, reminded her of that movie *Gremlins.* She'd
already logged over a dozen calls. Though what anyone
thought *we* could do about any of it was beyond her.
Was I on my way in?

Sure, I said.

New plan was (I told J. T.) we'd go in for an hour,
two at the most, and sand down the rough spots.

It took Lonnie, J. T., and me well into the afternoon
to get everyone calmed down and the town more or
less back on track. House calls included the local
retirement home, where one of the cicadas had somehow got down a resident's mouth and choked her to
death; a little girl terrified that the bugs were going to
eat her newborn kittens; and a Mr. Murphy living
alone in an old house I'd thought long abandoned.
Neighbors having heard screams, J. T. and I arrived to
find that Mr. Murphy had intimate knowledge of
insects: when we lifted him from his wheelchair, mag-
gots writhed in ulcers the size of saucers on his but-
tocks, some of them dropping to the floor, and more
could be seen at work in the cushions and open frame-
work of the chair. "Don't much mind the littluns," he
said, looking from J. T.'s face to mine. "Them big ones

is a different story altogether."

So the *new* new plan was to get a late lunch, then head up into the hills. And since chances were good we might not be out of there by nightfall, I'd look up Nathan first. No way I was going to be in those hills after dark without someone who knew them.

Chapter Nineteen

We parked by the derelict cotton gin and came up the line of humps and hollows that form the mountain's side, an easier but much longer ascent. By the time we reached the cabin, it was going on four o'clock. The owner didn't take too much to yard work. Every couple of years he'd clear a space around the cabin. The rest of the time pine trees, shrubs, and bushes, along with a variety of grasses and wildflowers, had their way. We were well along into the rest of the time.

Nathan stepped out from behind an oak, twelve-gauge in the crook of an elbow. His dog came out from beneath the cabin growling, then, at Nathan's almost silent whistle, went back under.

"Defending the realm?" I asked.

"Been out."

"Hunting?"

"After a fashion."

Meeting J. T.'s eye, he said, "Miss." I introduced them. "Found the camp," he went on, "maybe three miles in, 'bout forty degrees off north-northeast. Ain't much to it, mostly the hind end of a cabin they done put some lean-tos up against."

"How many are there?"

"If you mean lean-tos, there's three. If you're asking after people, which I expect you are, then my guess'd be close on to a dozen. Youngsters was all I saw. You headin' up that way?"

I nodded. "Talk you into coming along?"

"Figured to."

Instinctively tilting the shotgun barrel maybe ten degrees to clear a low branch, Nathan stepped back into the trees.

It took us almost two hours to get there. By the time we did, the sun had put in its papers and was marking time. The lean-tos were saplings lashed together with heavy twine, a spool of which I later saw inside what was left of the original cabin. The cabin hadn't been much to start with. Now it came down to half a room, five-sixths of a chimney, and a smatter of roof. A smatter of people sat on a bench out front—more saplings, these set into notches in two sections of log.

One of the homesteaders, a woman like all of them in her early to late twenties, sat beside a pile of sassafras root, cleaning with a damp cloth what was to be a new addition to the pile. Another was picking through field greens. They watched us silently as we approached. A man emerging from one of the lean-tos paused, then straightened and stepped towards us. Another, that I'd not seen and damn well should have, swung down off the low branch of a maple at the edge of the clearing. Scraps of plank from the cabin were nailed to the trunk at intervals to make a ladder.

Boards had also been nailed up over the cabin's gaping front, three of them, bridging the void. Crude block letters in white paint: "All the Whys Are Here."

"Tell me you're not the trouble you look to be," the man from the lean-to said, holding out his hand, which I shook. Older than the rest, pushing thirty from the far side, dark eyes, beetle brow, bad skin.

"Deputy sheriff," I said, "but not trouble. Not the kind you're thinking, at any rate."

"Always good to hear. Isaiah Stillman." Nodding towards Nathan, who stood apart at clearing's edge, he said, "Your friend's welcome, too."

"My friend's not much for company."

"Um-hmm. He the one lives down the mountain?"

"The same."

"So what can we do for you, Deputy? If we're—" He stopped, eyes meeting mine. "Our understanding is that this is free land."

"Close as it gets these days, anyhow."

I described the young man who'd died by the lake last night, told Stillman how it happened.

"I'm truly sorry to hear that."

"You knew him, then?"

"Of course. Kevin. We wondered where he'd got off to this time. Never could stay in place too long. He'd go off, be gone a day or two, a week. But he'd always come back."

The woman cleaning sassafras had put rag and roots down and walked up behind Stillman, touching him on the shoulder. When he turned, her mouth moved, but no sound came. Taking her hand and placing it against his throat, he said: "It's Kevin, Moira. Kevin's dead." Her mouth opened and went round in a silent *no*. After a moment she returned to the bench and her work. The other woman there put a hand briefly to her cheek.

"We'll be having our dinner soon," Stillman said. "Will you join us?"

We did, settling into a meal of lukewarm sassafras tea, greens, rice cooked with black-eyed peas—

"Our take on hopping John," Stillman said.

"Interesting."

"Flavored with roots instead of salt pork or bacon, since we're vegetarians."

—and something that must have been hoecake,

which, like hopping John, I'd read and heard about but never seen.

"Delicious."

J. T. cocked eyebrows at me at that. Nathan, having got over his standoffishness, was busy sopping up juice from the greens with crumbly bits of hoecake.

"We plan to grind our own cornmeal eventually," Stillman said.

Of course they did.

"I should notify your friend's family," I said. Helped myself to another spoonful of the hopping John. Stuff kind of grew on you.

"We *are* his family, Mr. Turner."

"No direct relatives?"

"His father threw him out of the house when he was fourteen. 'The old man was an engineer,' Kevin always said. 'He knew how things were supposed to work.' For a year or two he stayed around town. His mother would meet him, give him money. When she died, Kevin left for good."

"What about the rest of you?"

"Have family, you mean."

"Yes."

"Some of us do, some don't. For us, family is—"

Leaning over the makeshift table, the young woman I assumed to be deaf and dumb moved her hands in dismissive, sweep-it-away gestures.

"Moira's right," Stillman said.

"You always *think* she is," one of the others said.

He ignored that. "This isn't the time to be talking about such. Besides, night's closing in. I imagine you'll be wanting to get back."

"We should, yes."

"You and your friends are always welcome here… Can you see to Kevin's burial, or should we?"

"We can do that."

"We'd expect to pay for it, of course."

"The county—"

"It's our responsibility. We do have money."

We both looked about the camp, then realized what we were doing, looked at one another, and smiled.

"Really," he said. "It's not a problem—despite appearances. So we'll be expecting an invoice. Meanwhile, you have our gratitude."

Moira raised a hand in farewell. Nathan, J. T., and I stepped out to the accompaniment of a half moon and the calls of whippoorwills, down hills and across them, right and left legs lengthening alternately like those of cartoon figures to meet the challenge, or so it seemed, returning to a world gone strange in our absence.

Chapter Twenty

"I know almost nothing about you."

Her eyes went from my eyes to my mouth and back, ever steady.

"Why should you?"

Outside, rain slammed down, turning lawns and walkways to patches of mud. A mockingbird crouched in the window, soaked feathers drawn tightly about.

"I come here every week for—what? a year now?— and we talk. Most of my relationships haven't lasted near that long."

I let that go by.

"I know almost nothing about you. And you know so much about me."

"Only what you've agreed to have me know, or what you've told me yourself."

"Here's something you don't know. When I was a

child, ten or so…" For a moment she drifted away. "I had this friend, Gerry. And I had this T-shirt I'd sent away for, off some cereal box or out of a comic book. Nothing special, now that I think about it, just this thin, cheap shirt, blue, with 'Wonder Girl' stenciled on it in yellow letters. But I loved that T-shirt. I'd waited by the mailbox every day till it came. My mother had to take it out of my room at night while I was sleeping, just to wash it… It was summer, and all day there'd been a rain, like this one. Then late afternoon it slowed, still coming down, but more a shower now. Gerry starts running down the drive and sliding into this huge mud puddle at its end. This is back in Georgia, we didn't have paving, just a dirt drive cut in from the street. At first I didn't want to, but I tried it, then… just gave myself to the simple joy of it. Gerry and I went on sliding and diving for most of the rest of the afternoon. My shirt was ruined, of course. Mother tried everything to get it clean. The last I saw of it, it was in with the rags."

She looked back from the window.

"Poor thing."

"The bird?"

She nodded. Muffled conversation came from the hall, indecipherable, rhythmic. It sounded much like the rain outside.

"You must have to turn in some sort of reports," she said.

"I do."

"In which case, it has to be coming up on time for one."

After a moment I said, "They're not going to give your license back, Miss Blake."

She looked at the watch, which from old habit she still wore pinned to her shirt pocket. "I know. I do know that... And I've asked you to call me Cheryl." She smiled. "Recently I've taken up reading again. Do you know the science fiction writer Philip K. Dick?"

"A little."

"Late in life, while visiting in Canada, he underwent some kind of crisis, something like Poe's last days, maybe. He came to in a fleabag hotel and had himself committed to a detox center. Another patient there told a story that promptly became Dick's favorite slogan. This junkie goes to see his old friend Leon, and once he gets to his friend's house he asks the people there if he can see Leon. 'I'm very sorry to have to tell you this,' one of them says, 'but Leon is dead.' 'No problem,' the junkie responds, 'I'll just come back on Thursday.'"

She stood.

"See you on Thursday."

Long after she was gone—my next client had canceled—I sat quietly. Eventually the rain lightened and, with a vigorous shake of feathers, the mockingbird launched itself from the window.

As an RN on a cancer ward, Cheryl Blake, who now worked as a cosmetics salesperson, had drawn up morphine and injected it through the IV ports of at least three patients. At trial, asked if the patients had told her they wished to die, her response was: "They didn't need to. I knew." She served six years. Two days before Christmas last year, the state had paroled her. I saw her first on New Year's Eve.

Memory opens on small hinges. A prized T-shirt long ago lost. The pale green chenille bedspread, its knots worn to nubbins, I'd had as a child and sat night after night in my cell remembering. I'd gone in, in fact, on New Year's Eve.

In prison, trees are always far away. From the yard you could look across to a line of them like a mirage on the horizon, so distant and unreal that they might as well have been on another planet. They were bare then, of course, just gray smudges of trunk and limb against the lighter gray of sky. When springtime came, their green was a wound.

In a corner of the yard that spring, Danny Lillo planted seeds from an apple his daughter brought him. Each day he'd dip the ladle into the tank that provided our drinking water on the yard, fill his mouth, and take it over to that corner. Week after week we watched. Saw that first long oval of a leaf ease from the ground, watched as the third set of leaves developed pointy tips. Then we went out one afternoon and someone had pulled it up. Maybe four inches long, it lay there on its side, trailing roots. Danny stood looking down a long time. All of us who had given up so much already, the one who put it in the ground, those who simply watched and waited, the one who pulled it up—all of us had lost something we couldn't even define, all of us felt something that, like so much else in that gray place, had no name.

Chapter Twenty-One

Back here in the world, so strange and so familiar at the same time, this was my life. No sign of insight or epiphany peeking through floorboards, sound track of my days innocent of all but the din of memories going round and round. One longs for the three chords of a Hank Williams song to nose it all into place.

The short list was this: an old cabin I had every intention of fixing up, a job I'd blundered into, a clutch of friends likewise unintended. And Val. She was intended. Maybe not at first, but later on.

And always, the simple fact that I'd survived.

Miss Emily was happy to have me back, I'm pretty sure. The young ones were now getting around all too well on their own, straying into every corner of the cabin, not that the house had many corners, or that we could ever fail to locate them by their squeals. Val, in underpants and a faded Riley Puckett T-shirt, was asleep on the couch. When I kissed her she looked up at me blankly, focused for a moment to tell me "J. T. had a call," then plunged back asleep. Her briefcase was on the kitchen table. Labels of folders peeked above the edge. The Whyte Laydie banjo case sat on the floor beside the table.

"They want me back," J. T. said, coming in off the porch after returning the call. "Couple of federal marshals paid a call to a gentleman at a motel out on St. Louis Avenue and got themselves blown away for their trouble. All hell's broke loose."

She took a glass off the drying rack and poured from the bottle before me, sat down at the table. Emily strode in again to check on us, snout worrying the air. Pesky offspring are bad enough. She's expected to keep track of us as well?

"I told them no way."

"You sure about that?"

"I'm sure. You mind?"

"Not in the least. It's good to have you around."

"Same here."

I poured again for both of us. "Listen."

The outside door was open and she looked that way, through the screen. "To what?"

Exactly. Too quiet. Not even frogs. Of course, it was altogether possible that I'd just grown paranoid.

At any rate, we sat there, had another drink, and nothing came of it. When J. T. went off to bed, I got the Whyte Laydie from its case and took it outside, to the back porch. Touched fingers gently to strings, remembering the songs my father played and his father before him, "Pretty Polly," "Mississippi Sawyer," "Napoleon Crossing the Rhine," remembering, too, my father's touch. The strings went on ringing long after I'd raked a finger across them.

"I had," Isaiah Stillman would tell me on my second visit, as J. T. and Moira sat getting silently acquainted on the bench, "the overwhelming sense that my life was a book I'd only skimmed—one that deserved, for all its apparent insignificance, actually to be read. Meanwhile, my grandmother was dying. We'd moved away and I never had the chance to know her. I went there, moved in with her—rural Iowa, a farmhouse in a place called Sharon Center, four houses and a garage, few besides Amish anywhere around—and saw her through her final days."

Holding the Whyte Laydie close, I sat remembering my own grandmother who in my shallow youth had refused to acknowledge the cancer that all too soon took her, commanding Grandfather to walk behind so he could tell her if her dresses showed traces of blood. What did I have of her? A few brief memories, blurred by time. Grandfather I got to know when he came to live with us afterwards. Neither of my parents showed much interest in anything he had to say. I on the other hand was fascinated by his stories, in thrall to them.

"At the end, she went into a hospital in Iowa City," Stillman said. "Not what she wanted, but there were other considerations. Standing there by her bed, I watched the tracings of the EKG monitor, the hillocks it made one after another, and I saw them as ripples, ripples going out into the world, becoming waves, waves that would go on and on and in a way would never end."

My grandparents had a country store. Ancient butcher block in the back, cooler full of salt pork, bacon, and other such cheap cuts of meat, an array of candy bars in one glass-front cabinet, another of toiletries and the like, worn wooden shelves of canned goods stacked in pyramids, the inevitable soft-drink machine with the caps of Coke, Pepsi, Nehi grape, and chocolate drink bottles peering up at you. You slid the desired drink along steel slats where it hung from its neck, into the gate, and dropped in your dime. Summers, when I spent a week or two with them, they let me work in the store. I'd hand over Baby Ruths, loaves of white bread, tubes of toothpaste, and squat jars of Arid deodorant, collect money, hit the key that so satisfyingly opened the register, make change. Most of our customers were black folk working on farms nearby. Afternoons, the white owners would come in, help themselves to a soft drink, and sit gossiping with my grandfather.

"You mentioned other considerations," I said to Stillman.

"Local family members. Despite her mode of life, they were convinced—a longtime family legend—that Gram had squirreled away huge sums of money."

Seeing me glance towards her, Moira lifted her hand in a sketchy wave. Moments later J. T. did the same.

"Funny thing is, she had, literally," Stillman said. "Almost a million. By then she'd given a lot of it away. Imagine how pissed they were."

I did and, petty human being that I am, rather enjoyed doing so.

"What was left went into a foundation that I still oversee."

"Without electricity or phone service?"

"Batteries. Satellites. A laptop."

"What a world it's become."

"Same way I went about finding others like myself. It took a great while. Whereas, before, it would have been hit-and-miss at best." He stood and walked to clearing's edge, after a moment turned back. "My grandmother was twelve when she got off the train at Auschwitz. A child, though she would not be a child much longer. She survived. Her parents and two siblings didn't."

Folding back the sleeve of his shirt, he revealed the numbers that stood out on the muscles of his forearm. "It's as exact a reproduction as I could manage. Many of us have them."

Chapter Twenty-Two

The cicadas were gone. Val lost two cases, won another, went on the Internet to pull down tablatures of "Eighth of January" and "Cluck Old Hen." The reek of magnolia was everywhere, and single-winged maple seeds coptered down on our heads—or was that earlier? Lonnie resigned. "Thing is, Turner, I don't do it now, I'm never going to." Eldon had a new guitar, a Stella with a pearloid fingerboard from the thirties in which someone had installed a pickup. "Not collectible anymore, but it still has that great old sound." J. T. sat on the porch tapping feet, drinking ice tea, and saying maybe this time-off thing wasn't so bad after all. Don Lee was out of the hospital, making the two-hour drive to Bentonville three days a week for rehab. He'd tried coming back to work a few hours a day. Second week of it, June pulled me aside. He and I had a talk that afternoon. I told him he was one of the best I'd ever worked with. But you don't have to do this anymore, I said. You know that, right? He sat looking out the window, shaking his head. It's not that I don't want to, Turner, he said. With all that's happened, I want to more than ever. I just don't know if I can.

No further foul winds came blowing down out of Memphis.

Patently, I was an alarmist.

Town life went on. Brother Tripp from First Baptist was seen peering into cars at one of the local parking spots popular among teenagers. Barry and Barb shut down the hardware store after almost twenty years. Customers routinely made the forty-mile drive to WalMart now, they said, and, anyway, they were tired. Thelma quit the diner. Sally Johnson, last year's prom queen, promptly took her spot. Slow afternoons, I'd give a try to imagining Thelma's existence away from waitressing. What would her house or apartment look like, and what would she do there all day? Did she wear that same sweater distorted by so many years of tips weighing down one pocket? Robert Poole from the feed store left his wife and four children. Melinda found the note on the kitchen table when she came home from a late shift at Mitty's, the town's beauty shop. *Took the truck. The rest is yours. Love, Rob.*

Everyone in town knew what happened up there in

the hills, of course, and reactions were mixed, long-bred suspicion of outsiders, youth, and those demonstrably different tripping tight on the heels of declarations of What a shame about that boy! When the funeral came round, Isaiah Stillman and his group filed down from their camp, sat quietly through the ceremony, then got up quietly and left. More than a dozen townspeople also attended.

When Val told me she was thinking about quitting her job, I said she was too damned young for a midlife crisis.

"Eldon's asked me to go on the road with him."

"What, covering the latest pap out of Nashville? How proud I am to be a redneck, God bless the U.S.A.?"

"Quite the opposite, actually. He's bought a trailer, plans on living in it, travelling from one folk or blue-grass festival to the next, playing traditional music."

Buy an eighty-year-old guitar, that's the sort of thing that can happen to you, I guess. Suddenly you're no longer satisfied working roadhouses for a living.

"You've no idea how many there are," Val said. "I know I didn't. Hundreds of them, all across the country. We'd be doing old-time Ballads, mountain music, Carter Family songs."

No doubt they'd be an arresting act. Black R&B man out of the inner city, white banjo player with a law degree from Tulane. Joined to remind America of its heritage.

"I wouldn't expect to take the Whyte Laydie, of course."

"You should, it's yours. My grandfather would be pleased to know that it's still being played."

"And how very much it's revered?"

"He might have some trouble getting his head around that. Back then, he most likely ordered it from the local general store, paid a dollar or two a week on it. Instruments were tools, like spades or frying pans. Something to help people get by."

We were out on the porch, me leaning against the wall, Val with feet hanging off the side. Bright white moon above. Insects beating away at screens and exposed skin.

Val said, "I'd never have come to this place in my life without you, you know."

"Right."

"I mean it."

I sat beside her. She took my hand.

"You have no idea how well you fit in here, do you? Or how many people love you?"

I knew *she* did, and the thought of losing her drove pitons through my heart. Climbers scrambled for purchase.

"This is not just something you're thinking about, then."

She shook her head.

"I'll miss you."

Leaning against me there in the moonlight, she asked, "Do I really need to say anything about that?"

No.

She stood. "I'm going to spend the last few days at the house shutting it down. Who knows, maybe someday I'll actually complete the restoration."

I saw her to the Volvo and returned to my vigil on the porch, soon became aware of a presence close by. The screen door banged gently shut behind her as J. T. stepped out.

"She told you, huh?"

"A heads-up would have been good."

"Val asked me not to say anything. I don't think she was sure, herself, right up till now. Amazing moon." She had a bottle of Corona and passed it to me. I took a swig. "Talked to my lieutenant today."

Hardly a surprise. The department was calling daily in its effort to lure her back. Demands had given way to entreaty, appeals to her loyalty, barely disguised bribes, promises of promotion.

"Be leaving soon, then?"

"Not exactly." She finished the beer and set the bottle on the floorboards. "You didn't want the sheriff's position, right?"

"Lonnie's job? No way.

"Good. Because I met with Mayor Sims today, and I took it."

Chapter Twenty-Three

Obviously it was my time for surprises. And for mixed feelings. Wounded at the thought of Val's departure, nonetheless I was pleased that she'd be doing what she most loved. The two emotions rode a teeter-totter, one rising, the other touching feet to earth—before they reversed.

And J. T.? As my boss? Well…

I gave some thought to how she, city-bred and a city-trained officer, would fit in here. But then I remembered the way she and Moira had sat together up in the hills and decided she'd do okay. It goes without saying how pleased I was that she'd be around.

I was considerably less pleased when Miss Emily chewed a hole in the screen above the sink and took her brood out through it.

Because I considered it a betrayal? Because it was yet

another loss? Or simply because I would miss them?

I was standing in the kitchen, staring at the hole in the screen, when J. T. swung by to see if I wanted to grab some dinner. She had moved into a house on Mulberry, or, more precisely, into one room. The house had been empty a long time, and the rest would take a while. But the price was right. Her monthly rent was about what a couple in the city might spend on a good dinner out.

"They're wild animals, Dad, not pets. What, you expected her to leave a note?"

"You think she moved in just to be sure her off-spring would be safe? Knowing all along she'd leave afterwards?"

"Somehow I doubt possums very often overplan things."

"I thought…" Shaking myself out of it: "I don't know what I thought."

"So. Dinner?"

"Not tonight. You mind?"

"Of course not."

Some time after she left, second bourbon slammed down and coffee brewing, the perfect response came to me: But we slept together, you know, Miss Emily and I.

Rooting through stacks of CDs and tapes on shelves in the front room, I found what I was looking for.

It had been one of those drawling, seemingly end-less Sunday afternoons in May. We'd grilled chicken and burgers earlier and were dipping liberally, ad lib as Val kept insisting, into the cooler for beers, bolstering such excursions with chips, dip, carrot sticks, and potato salad scooped finger-style from the bowl. Eldon sprang open the case on his Gibson, Val went inside to get the Whyte Laydie, and they started playing. I'd recently had the cassette recorder out for something or another and set it up on the windowsill in the kitchen. Just about where Miss Emily and crew went through.

"Keep on the Sunny Side," "White House Blues," "Frankie and Albert." No matter that lyrics got scram-bled, faked, or lost completely, the music kept its power.

"We should do this more often," Val said as they took a break. I'd left the recorder running.

"We should do this all the time." Eldon held up his jelly glass, half cranberry juice, half club soda, in salute. Only Val and I were dipping into the cooler.

Soon enough they were back at it.

"Banks of the Ohio," "Soldier's Joy," "It Wasn't God Who Made Honky-Tonk Angels."

I left the tape going and went back out onto the porch. Just days ago I'd been thinking how full the house was. Now suddenly everyone was gone. Even Miss Emily. Val and Eldon shifted into "Home on the

Range," Eldon, playing slide on standard guitar, doing the best he could to approximate Bob Kaai's Hawaiian steel.

"What the hell is that you're listening to?" a voice said. "No wonder someone wants you dead, you piti- ful fuck."

Diving forward, I kicked the legs out from under the chair and he, positioned behind with the steel-wire garrote not quite in place yet, went along, splayed across the chair's back. An awkward position. Before he had the chance to correct it, I pivoted over and had an arm locked around his neck, alert to any further sound or signs of intrusion. The garrote, piano wire with tape-wound wood handles, sat at porch's edge looking like a garden implement.

"Simple asphyxiation," Doc Oldham said an hour later.

I do remember pulling the arm in hard, asking if he was alone, getting no answer and asking again. Was he contract? Who sent him? No response to those ques- tions either. Then the awareness of his body limp beneath me.

"Man obviously didn't care to carry on a conversa- tion with you," Doc Oldham said, grabbing hold of the windowsill to pull himself erect with difficulty, totter- ing all the way up and tottering still once there. "'S that coffee I smell?"

"Used to be, anyway. Near dead as this guy by now's my guess."

"Hey, it's late at night and I'm a doctor. You think I'm so old I forgot my intern days? Bad burned coffee's diesel fuel for us—what I love most. Next to a healthy slug of bourbon."

Meanwhile J. T. waited, coming to the realization that further black-and-whites would not be barreling up, that there were no fingerprint people or crime lab investigators to call in, no watch commander to pass things off to. It was all on her.

She sat at the kitchen table. Doc nodded to her and said "Asphyxiation," poured his coffee and took the glass of bourbon I handed him.

"Tough first day," I said.

"Technically I haven't even started."

"Hope you had a good dinner at least."

"Smothered chicken special."

"Guess homemaking only goes so far."

"Give me a break, I'm still trying to find the kitchen. Speaking of which, this coffee really sucks."

"Don't pay her any mind, Turner," Doc Oldham said, helping himself to a second cup. "It's delicious."

"I'm assuming there's no identification," J. T. said.

"These guys don't exactly carry passports. There's better than a thousand dollars in a money clip in his left pants pocket, another thousand under a false insole in his shoe. A driver's license that looks like it was made yesterday."

"Which it probably was. So, we have no way to track where he might have been staying because there isn't any place to stay. And with no bus terminals or airports—"

"No airports? What about Stanley Municipal? Crop duster to the stars."

"—there's no paper trail." She sipped coffee and made a face. "Nothing I know is of any help here."

"What you *know* is rarely important. The rest is what matters—all those hours of working the job, interviews, people you've met, the instincts nurtured by all of it. That's what you use."

"Something you learned in psychology classes?"

"From Eldon, actually. Spend hours practicing scales and learning songs, he said, then you get up there to play and none of it matters. Where you begin and where you wind up have little to do with one another. Meanwhile we," I said, passing it over, "do have this."

I gave her a moment.

"Thing you have to ask is, this is a pro, right? First to last he covers his tracks. That's what he does, how he lives. No wallet, false ID if any at all, he's a ghost, a glimmer. So why does a stub from an airline ticket show up in his inside coat pocket?"

"Carelessness?"

"Possible, sure. But how likely?"

I was, after all, patently an alarmist, possibly para-noid, a man known to have accused a possum of over-planning.

It was only the torn-off stub of a boarding pass and easily enough could have been overlooked. You glance at aisle and seat number, stick it in your pocket just in case, find it there the next time you wear that coat.

But I wasn't running scales, I was up there on stage, playing. And judging from the light in J. T.'s eyes, she was too.

Chapter Twenty-Four

His name, or at least one of his names, was Marc Bruhn, and he'd come in on the redeye, nonstop, from Newark to Little Rock. Ticket paid in cash, round trip, no flags, whistles, or bells. These guys play everything close to the vest. Extrapolating arrival to service-desk time, despite false identification and despite Oxford, Mississippi, having been given as destination, J. T. was able to track a car rental.

"That's the ringer, what got me onto him. Who the hell, if he's heading for Oxford, would fly into Little Rock rather than Memphis?"

"Hey, he's from New Jersey, remember?"

We'd found the car under a copse of trees across the lake. There was a half-depleted six-pack of bottled water on the floorboard, an untouched carton of Little Debbie cakes on the passenger seat, and a self-improvement tape in the player.

June was able to pull out previous transactions in the name of Marc Bruhn, Mark Brown, Matt Browen, and other likely cognates. Newark International, JFK, and La Guardia; Gary, Indiana, and nearby Detroit; Oklahoma City, Dallas, Phoenix; Seattle, St. Louis, L.A.

"That's it, that's as far as my reach goes."

But good as J. T. and June proved to be, Isaiah Stillman was better.

"You told me you managed a conservatorship via the Internet," I said on a visit that evening. "And that's how you put all this together."

"Yes, sir." I'd asked him to stop the sir business, but it did no good. "I grew up limping, one leg snared forever in a modem. The Internet's the other place I live."

I told him about Bruhn, about the killings. We were dancing in place, I said, painting by numbers, since we were pretty sure who sent him. But we hadn't been able to get past a handful of basic facts and suspicions.

"We take the individual's right to privacy and autonomy very seriously, Mr. Turner."

"I know."

"On the other hand, we're in your debt. And however we insist upon holding ourselves apart from it, this community is one we've chosen to live in, which implies certain responsibilities."

Our eyes held, then his went to the trees about us:

the rough ladder, the treehouse built for children to come.

"Excuse me."

Entering one of the lean-tos, he emerged with a laptop.

"Moira tells me Miss Emily left," he said.

"And Val."

"Val will be back. Miss Emily won't. Marc, right? With a *c* or a *k?* B-R-U-H-N?" Fingers rippling on keys. "Commercial history—which you have already. List of Bruhns by geographical distribution, including alternate spellings… Here it is, narrowed down to the New Jersey–New York area… You want copies of any of this, let me know."

"I don't see a printer."

"No problem, I can just zap it to your office, right?"

Could he? I had no idea.

"Now for the real fun. I'm putting in the name… commercial transactions we know about… the Jersey–New York list… and a bunch of question marks. Like fishhooks." His fingers stopped. "Let's see what we catch."

Lines of what I assumed to be code snaked steadily down the screen. Nothing I could make any sense of.

"Here we go." Stillman hit a few more keys. "Looks as though your man advertises in a number of niche publications. Gun magazines, adventure publications and the like. Not too smart of him."

"The smart criminals are all CEOs."

"No Internet presence that I can—" Stillman's hands flashed to the keyboard. "There's a watcher."

I shook my head.

"A sentinel, a special kind of firewall. The question marks I put in, the fishhooks—that was like opening up a gallery of doors. We were entering one when the alarm triggered. I hit the panic button pretty quickly, so chances are good the watcher never got a fix on me. Probably be best if I stayed offline a while, all the same." He shut the computer off and lowered the lid. "Sorry. Have a cup of tea before you go?"

We sat on the bench, everyone else gone to bed by this time. I held the mug up close, breathing in the rich aroma, loving the feel of the steam on my face. Stillman touched me on the shoulder and pointed to the sky as a shooting star arced above the trees. *Big star fallin, mama ain't long fore day… Maybe the sunshine'll drive my blues a-way.* My eyes dropped to the boards nailed up over the cabin and the legend thereon. Stillman's eyes followed.

"I've been meaning to ask you about that."

"It went up the moment we moved in." He sipped his tea with that strange intensity he gave most everything—as though this might be the last cup of tea he'd ever drink. "From my grandmother's life, like so much else."

Bending to lift the teapot off the ground (ceramic, thrown by Moira, lavender-glazed), he refilled our mugs.

"*Hier ist kein Warum.* A guard told her that on her first morning at the camp as he brought her a piece of stale bread. There is no *why* here. In his own way, she said, he was being kind."

Mind tumbling with thoughts of kindness and cruelty and the ravage of ideas, I struck out for my newly empty house, fully confident of finding the way without a guide now, though once I could have sworn I saw Nathan off in the trees watching to be sure I made it out all right. Imagined, of course. That same night I also thought I saw Miss Emily in the yard, which could have been only the shadow of a limb: wind and moonlight in uneasy alliance to take on substance.

Chapter Twenty-Five

Herb Danziger called that morning to tell me the execution had been carried out and Lou Winter was dead. I thanked him. Herb said come see him sometime before he and his nurse ran away together. I asked how long that would be and he said it probably better be soon. I hung up, and had no idea what I felt.

I sat thinking about a patient I had back in Memphis. He'd come in that first time wearing a five-hundred-dollar suit, silk tie, and cordovan shoes so highly polished it looked as though he were walking on two violins. "Harris. Just the one name. Don't use any others." He shook hands, sat in the chair, and said, "Ammonia."

"I'm sorry?"

"Ammonia."

I looked around.

"Not here. Well, yes: here. Everywhere, actually. That's the problem."

Light from the window behind bled away his features. I got up to draw the blinds.

"Everywhere," he said again as I took my seat. His eyes were like twin perched crows.

Eight and a half weeks before, as he rummaged about in stacks of file boxes in the basement looking through old papers, the smell of ammonia had come suddenly upon him. There was no apparent source for it; he'd checked. But the smell had been with him ever since. He'd seen his personal physician, then by referral an internist, an allergist, and an endocrinologist. Now he was here.

I asked the obvious question, which is mostly what therapists do: What papers had he been looking for? He brushed that aside in the manner of a man long accustomed to ignoring prattle and attending to practicalities, and went on talking about the stench, how sometimes it was overpowering, how other times he could almost pretend that it had left him.

From session to session over a matter of weeks, as in stop-motion, I watched dress and demeanor steadily deteriorate. That first appointment had been set by a secretary. When, a couple of months in, with an emergency on my hands, I tried to call to cancel a session, I learned that Harris's phone had been disconnected.

The poise and punctuality of early visits gave way to tardiness and to disjunctive dialogue that more and more resembled a single, ongoing monologue. When he paused, he was not listening for my response but for something from within himself. Trains of thought left the station without him. He began to (as a bunkmate back in country had said of the company latrines) not smell so good.

The last time I saw him he peered wildly around the corner of the open door, came in and took his seat, and said, "I've been shot by the soldiers of Chance."

I waited.

"Not to death, I think—not quite. Casualties are grave, though."

He smiled.

"I'm bleeding, Captain. Don't know if I can make it back to camp." As he smiled again, I recalled his eyes that first time, the alertness in them, the resolve. "It was a report card," he said.

Not understanding, I shook my head.

"What I was looking for in the basement. It was a report card from the eighth grade, last one before graduation. Three years in junior high and I had all As, but some of the teachers put their busy heads together and decided that wasn't such a good idea. I got my report card in its little brown envelope, opened it, and there were two B-pluses, history and math. Just like that."

"I'm sorry."

"Sorry. Yeah… You know what I did? I laughed. I'd always suspected the world wasn't screwed down so well. Now I had proof."

After he left, I sat thinking. The world's an awfully big presence to carry a grudge against, but so many people do just that. Back in prison, the air was thick with such grudges, so thick you could barely breathe, barely make your way through the corridors, men's lives crushed to powder under the weight. On the other hand, maybe that was a part of what had motivated Harris all these years. But it gave out, quit working, the way things do.

Just over a week later, I was notified that Harris had been picked up by police and remanded by the courts to the state hospital. Declaring that he had no family, he'd given my name. I had the best intentions of going to see him, but before I could, he broke into the janitor's supply room and drank most of a can of Drano.

"You okay, Deputy?"

I pushed back from the desk and swiveled my chair around. J. T. had taken to calling me that of late. What began as a passing joke, stuck. I told her about Lou Winter. She came over and put her hand on my arm.

"I'm sorry, Dad."

Her other hand held a sheaf of printouts.

"So Stillman *was* able to zap it here."

"It's not magic, you know."

To this day I remain unconvinced of that. But I spent most of two hours bent over those sheets, trying to find something in them that Stillman had missed, some corner or edge sticking out a quarter-inch, any possible snag, and remembering what one of my teachers back in college used as an all-purpose rejoinder. You'd come in with some grand theory you'd sewn together and she'd listen carefully. Then when you were done, she'd say, "Random points of light, Mr. Turner. Random points of light."

Around eleven I took my random points of light and the butt that usually went along with them down to the diner. The raging controversy of the day seemed to be whether or not the big superstore out on the highway to Poplar Bluff was ever really going to open. The lot had been paved and the foundation laid months ago, walls like massive jigsaw parts started going up, then it all slammed to a stop—because the intricate webwork of county payoffs and state kickbacks had somehow broken down, most believed. I sat over my coffee listening to the buzz around me and noticing how everything outside the window looked bleached out, as though composed of only two colors, both of them pale. But that was me, not the light.

Where had I read *the broken bottles our lives are?*

"You hear about Sissy Coopersmith yet?"

Sy Butts slid into the booth across from me. He'd been wearing that old canvas hunting jacket since he was a kid, everyone said. Now Sy was pushing hard at sixty. Pockets meant to hold small game were long gone; daylight showed here and there like numerous tiny doorways.

I shook my head.

Sally brought his coffee and refilled my cup for the third or fourth time.

"You know as how she was working as a nurse's aide, going from house to house taking care of the elderly? Had a gift for it, some said. Well, she'd been saving up her money for this seminar down West Memphis way. Last week's when it was. Got on the bus Friday morning and no one's heard a word since... Kind of surprised Lon and Sandra ain't been in to see you."

"She's, what, twenty-five, twenty-six? Short of filing a missing-persons report, there's not a lot they can do."

"Never was much they could do, with that girl. Sweet as fresh apple cider, but she had a mind of her own."

"Some would say that's a good thing."

"Some'll say just about any damn thing comes to 'em."

Doc Oldham passed by outside the window and, catching my eye, did a quick dance step by way of greeting. Then, inexplicably, he leveled one finger at me, sighting along it.

Sy looked at Doc, then at me. I shrugged. Sy told me more about Sissy's having a mind of her own.

Doc Oldham walked in the door of the cabin that night half an hour after I did. No knock, and for some reason I'd failed to hear him coming, which was quite a surprise considering the old banger Ford pickup he'd been driving since Nixon and McCarthy were bosom buddies.

"Man works up a thirst on the road," he said.

I poured whiskey into a jelly glass and handed it to him. The glasses, with their rims and bellies, had been under the sink when I bought the place. I hadn't seen jelly glasses since leaving home.

"So what brings you all the way out here?"

He downed the bourbon in a single swallow, peered into the glass at the drop, like a lens, left behind.

"Here to do your physical."

"You're joking."

"Nope. Regulations say twice a year. When'd we do your last one?"

"We didn't."

"Exactly."

I'd learned long ago that, for all his seeming insouciance, once Doc got something in his mind it stayed there. So as he pulled various instruments from the old carpetbag ("A real one, from right after the war. Some good ol' boys shot the original owner down in Hattiesburg") I pulled myself, per instruction, out of most of my clothes.

Somehow, as he poked and prodded at me and mumbled to himself, we both got through it, me with the help of well-practiced fortitude, Doc with the help of my bourbon. "Not bad," he said afterwards, "for a man of... oh, whatever the hell age you are. Watch what you eat, drink less"—this, as he dumped what was left of the bottle into his jelly glass—"and you might think about taking up a hobby, something that requires physical exertion. Like dancing."

"Dancing, huh?"

"Yep."

"Would carrying an old man outside and throwing him in the lake count?"

He considered. "Well, of course, for it to be of benefit, you'd have to do it repetitively." He threw the stethoscope and reflex hammer into the bag, then, noticing that the blood-pressure cuff was still on my arm, unwrapped that and threw it in too. "Day or two, I'll fetch a copy of my report round to the office. Take a little longer for the lab work, have to send that over to the hospital at Greer's Bay. Used to run the blood myself, but just don't have the patience for it anymore."

Doc started for the door, light on his feet as ever: the cabin walls shook.

"This had to be done today, right?"

He turned. "Fit things in when I can."

"Sure you do."

Our eyes met. Neither of us said anything for a moment.

"I heard Val might be pulling up stakes."

"Guess there's no 'might' to it. Just do me a favor, Doc: don't ask me what I feel about this, okay?"

"Wouldn't think of it. Sorry, though."

The walls shook a little more. I looked through the screen door and saw him sitting motionless in the truck. Then I heard the old Ford cough and gasp its way into life. I listened as it wound down the road and around the lake.

The phone rang not too long after. I took my time getting in off the porch. Thing quit about the time I got to it, then started up again as I was pouring a drink to carry back out.

"You forgot the beeper," J. T. said when I answered.

"Hope you don't—"

"Never mind. Meet me at the camp."

"Stillman's, you mean."

"Right. We just got a call. A little confusing—but I think it was Moira."

Chapter Twenty-Six

Back before I came here, for reasons that still escape me—one of those random, pointless notions that sometimes overtake us, especially, it seems, in middle age—I went home. I suppose I shouldn't say home. Where I grew up, rather.

It had never been much of a town. Now it wasn't much of anything. Many of the stores along Main Street were boarded up. Outside others, owners sat in lawn chairs, heads moving slowly to follow as I made my way down the cracked WPA sidewalk opposite. Every second or third tie was missing from the railroad tracks, rails themselves overgrown. A spike lay nearby, alongside the dried-out, mummified skin of a lizard, and I bent to pick it up. Its weight, the solidity of it, seemed strangely out of place here in this fading, forsaken landscape. Only stumps of walls, like broken bottom teeth, remained of the Blue Moon Café, whose porch and mysterious inner reaches for the whole of my childhood had been inhabited by black men eating sandwiches red with barbeque sauce and drinking from squat bottles of soft drinks. Outside town, the country store in which my grandparents spent eighteen hours every day of their adult life had become, with a crude white cross nailed to the front, the Abyssinian Holy God Church.

I walked along the levee thinking of all the times I'd sat here with Al, the two of us silhouetted against the sky as the town carried on its business behind and below. Old folks still talked about the great flood of 1908, but the river had begun drying up long before the town did, and now a man, if he watched his footing, could pretty much walk across and never wet his belt.

Like myself, the town was falling slowly towards the center of the earth.

Why is it that so often we begin to define a thing—come to that desire, and to the realization of its uniqueness—only at the very moment it is irrevocably changing and passing from us?

My life at the cabin and in the town, for instance. My family.

J. T.

Val.

I wasn't thinking about it that day back by the river, naturally, since none of it had happened then, but I was definitely thinking about it the morning I stood on a hill looking down at Stillman's camp.

Another thing I was thinking about, both times, was that all my life, with my time in the jungle, my years on the street as a cop, prison days, psychiatric work, even the place I grew up—all my life I'd lived out of step and synch with the larger world, forever tottering on borders and fault lines. It wasn't that I chose to do so; that's simply where I wound up.

As a counselor, of course, I'd have been quick to point out that we *always* make our choices, and that not choosing was as much a choice as any other. Such homilies are, as much as anything else, the reason I'd quit. It's too easy once you learn the tricks. You start off believing that you're discovering a way of seeing the world clearly, but you're really only learning a language—a dangerous language whose very narrowness fools you into believing you understand why people do the things they do.

But we don't. We understand so little of anything.

Such as why anyone would want to cause the rack and wreckage I saw below me in bright moonlight.

J. T. came trodding up the hill, sliding a bit on the wet grass. I curbed my impulse to make smart remarks about city folk.

"What do you think?"

Pretty much what she did, at that point.

The kids were down below, sifting through the rubble. For all my best intentions I couldn't help but think of them that way. Smoke curled from the remains of the cabin and crossed the moon. They'd come straggling in not long after we arrived—all but Stillman, who after sending the rest off into the woods had stayed behind to confront the interlopers.

We didn't hear Nathan until he was almost beside us.

"Missing someone?"

He carried his shotgun in the crook of an arm, barrel broken. My father and grandfather always did the same.

"Boy's back in about a mile."

"He okay?"

Nathan looked down at what was left of the camp. "Will be. Have to splint that leg fore we move him."

J. T. and I exchanged glances. "You saw who did this?" she said.

Nathan nodded.

"Three of 'em. Watched the others head off and knew they'd be all right. The boy, one that sorta runs things—"

"Isaiah."

"Him and the ones did this, I followed them. Figured, push came to shove…" He lifted a shoulder, raising the gunstock an inch or two, then, without saying more, turned and stepped off into trees. We followed.

"No way you're out hunting in the middle of the night."

"Not usually."

I stopped, putting a hand on Nathan's shoulder. I doubt anyone had touched him for years. He looked down at my hand, probably as surprised as I was, but none of it showing on his face.

"I been watching out for them," he said. "One way or the other, you knew they'd be having some trouble."

"Watching them, huh." We went on up a steep slope and down into a hollow. I saw Isaiah Stillman ahead, propped against a fallen maple. Another body lay a few paces away. "Because of your dog. Killing that boy."

"Just started me thinking, all the trouble could come their way up here."

"Like this," J. T. said.

"Or worse. Yes, ma'am."

"Sheriff," Stillman said as we approached. "Are the rest okay?"

I nodded.

"That old fucker shot me," the other one said. It looked bad, but it wasn't. Nathan knew his distance and how much buckshot would disperse. The boy's pants were shredded and his lower body well bloodied and someone at the ER was going to be picking out shot with tweezers for a couple of hours, but the boy'd be back on his feet soon enough.

"Shut up," J. T. told him.

"There was three of them," Nathan said, "all of them youngsters. Figure his friends'll be on the way to hiding under their beds by now.

J. T. looked at me. "Not another message from Memphis, then." Which is what we'd both been thinking, though neither of us had said it.

"Guess not."

"They tried to make me fight them," Stillman said. "When I wouldn't, that enraged them."

"Took to beatin' on the boy some fierce. Mainly that one there."

As Nathan nodded his direction, the boy started to say something. J. T. kicked his foot.

"So you stopped them," I said.

Nathan nodded. Pulling his knife, he peeled a thick slice of bark from the fallen tree, then hacked some vines from a bush nearby. Three minutes later he had Isaiah's leg splinted. "Other one, I figure we just throw him in the truck."

"Or in one of the ravines," J. T. said.

Girl was definitely catching on.

Chapter Twenty-Seven

We took Isaiah and the boy called Sammy to Cahoma County Hospital, then picked up the other two and put them away in the cells for the night. Tomorrow they'd either be headed to Cahoma County detention themselves, or up to Memphis, depending on what Judge Gray decided. Both of them stank of old beer and a kind of fear they'd never known before. One set of parents came in, listened to what we told them, shook their heads, and left. The other, a single mother, asked what she needed to do. You could tell by the way she said it that she'd been asking herself the same question for a long time.

From over by Jefferson, the boys said. Been drinking at the game and after, just having fun, you know? You remember what that was like. Someone had told them about these weirdos playing Tarzan up in the hills and they decided to go check it out.

"Be a long time before they get their lives unbent again," J. T. said.

Maybe. Always amazing, though, how resilient human beings can be.

It was Moira who, as they all quit camp, grabbed the laptop and took it along. She sent an e-mail, "an IM" as J. T. explained to me, to an old friend back in Boston, who then placed a "landline" call to the office.

I was thinking about that later in the morning, about Moira and about people's resilience, when Eldon stopped by and asked me if I felt like taking a walk. J. T. was home trying to get some sleep. June was off at lunch with Lonnie, their lunches having gotten to be a regular weekly thing. I signed out on the board and grabbed the beeper. We headed crosstown, out past the old Methodist church into what used to be the Meador family's rich pastureland and was now mostly scrub.

"You okay with this?" Eldon said after a while.

"Val and you, you mean."

"What we're doing, yeah."

"I think it's great."

"Most people think we're crazy."

"That's because you are."

"Well…"

We stopped to watch a woodpecker worrying away

at a sapling the size of a broomstick.

"No way there's anything in there worth all that work," Eldon said. "We'll be back, you know."

"Sure you will. But it will never be the same."

"No. It won't."

He bent down and pulled a blade of grass, held it between his thumbs and blew across it. Making music even with that.

"Hard to pick up and go, harder than I thought. Never would have suspected it. All these years, all these places, this is the only place that's ever felt like home."

"Like you say, you'll be back."

"What about those others—think they'll be back?"

"Memphis?"

He nodded.

"Not much doubt about it."

At wood's edge a young bird staggered about, flapping its wings.

"Trying them on for size," Eldon said. "Like he has this feeling, he's capable of something amazing, even if he doesn't know what it is yet."

We started back towards town.

"Good you're okay with it, then."

"You and Val? Sure. The other…"

"That's the way of it. Violence is a lonesome thing, it gets inside you and sits in there calling out for more. But they had no right bringing it here."

"And there should be an end to it. A natural end, an unnatural one—*some* kind of end. How long does it have to go on?"

"You're asking a black man?"

"Good point."

As we walked back, he talked about his and Val's plans, such as they were. An old-time music festival up around Hot Springs, this big campout that got thrown every year down in Texas, a solid string of bluegrass and folk festivals running from California up to Seattle.

"That's where all the VW microbuses go to die," Eldon told me. "Regular elephant's graveyard of them, all along the coast. VW buses, plaid shirts, and old guys with straggly gray ponytails everywhere you look."

We stopped outside the office. June waved from inside. Eldon looked in.

"She doing okay?"

I nodded.

"And Don Lee?"

"Not quite so good."

"Yeah." He started away, then turned. "All that stuff about giving something back? I always thought that was crap."

"Mostly it is."

"Yeah. Well… Mostly, everything is."

Lonnie had come back to the office with June. The two of them plus Don Lee were all sitting with coffee.

Don Lee nodded. Lonnie raised his cup in invitation.

"Who made it?" I asked.

June smiled.

Safe, then.

"Don't worry, Turner," Lonnie said. "Happens to all of us as we grow older, that getting cautious thing. Starts off with the coffee, say, then before you know it you're wearing double shirts on a windy day and stuffing newspapers around your door."

"Maybe even have a silly little hat you wear to bed when you take your afternoon naps," June said, Lonnie giving his best "Who, me?" look in response.

They'd heard about most of what had taken place out at the camp. The rest, I filled them in on.

"So why the hell'd they trash the place?" Lonnie asked.

"Who knows? But it's pretty much destroyed."

"We should get a bunch of people together," June said. "Go up there and help them rebuild."

We all looked at her. She was right. Sympathy had been gathering in the town for some time, since the day of the funeral for the boy Nathan's dog had killed. The camp's destruction, along with June's urging, put that sympathy over the top. In ensuing months, furniture, lumber, clothing, household goods, and a lot of time and effort would go up into those hills, all of us the better for it.

Lonnie shook his head. "Just kids."

"Just kids."

"You must have thought…"

"Of course we did."

"Anything further on that?"

"Nothing substantial, no. Eldon and I were just talking about it, wondering how long this has to go on."

"Once it starts…" Lonnie got up and poured himself another cup of coffee. "Some of these families have grudges reaching back to the day the first caveman said 'Hey look at me, I can walk upright!' They don't know any other way."

"You have to cut the head off," Don Lee said, speaking for the first time. "You cut the head off, it dies."

Chapter Twenty-Eight

I'm going to skip ahead here, past Monday and Tuesday, to the aftermath.

The call from Memphis came on a bright morning, Wednesday. Unable to sleep, I'd been shuffling papers and creating unnecessary files since 3 a.m. I was looking out the window, watching Bill from the Gulf station teaching his kid to ride a bike down the middle of Cherry Street, when the phone rang. A spider had built a spectacular web in the corner of the window. The web and bright-colored joints of the spider's legs caught morning sunlight like prisms.

"Sheriff's office."

"Turner?"

"You got him."

"Sam Hamill here."

"Always a pleasure."

"Sure it is."

"I assume you're not calling just to say hello."

"Not hardly." He held his hand over the receiver for a moment—to speak offstage, as it were. Then he was back. "Thing is, something strange has just happened up this way."

"It usually does."

"I've got a body."

I waited.

"Two, actually. But only the one that matters. Man goes by the name of Jorge Aleché."

"When?"

"Some time between noon and four yesterday, him and the bodyguard. Why do you ask?"

"Curiosity. What is it exactly that I can do for you, Sam?"

"I don't suppose there's any chance you'd have been back in town, right?"

"None at all. Been a little busy down this way, too."

"So I heard." After a moment he added: "I spoke to Sheriff Bates. Sorry about the shooting. He said you got the one who did it, though."

"The one who pulled the trigger, anyway."

"Well, it looks like someone may have gone a little deeper in country, if you know what I mean. 'Bout as far in as you can go, matter of fact. You think that's what happened, Turner?"

"Possible."

"I tried calling the current sheriff, one J. T. Burke, and was told by… just a minute… Mabel? Do I have that right?"

"Mabel. Right."

"Told me the sheriff was off on official business and would return my call as soon as possible. Little before that, I tried someone named Don Lee—"

"Acting sheriff."

"What I was told. So there's this Mabel person, secretary by the name of June, two or three sheriffs that I know of. You got one hell of a staff for a town that size."

"We take turns. Monday's my day as crossing guard."

"Sure it is. Anyway, the wife said this Don Lee was under the weather—recently sustained some injuries, I understand?—and was resting, and unless it was really important she didn't want to disturb him."

"Is there a message I can give Sheriff Burke for you, Sam?"

"What it comes down to is, since no one else seems to be available, here I am talking to you."

"Likewise."

"In an official capacity."

"Hold on then, let me get my badge and gun."

What sounded suspiciously like a snort came over

the line. "Never change, do you?"

"All the time."

"Given the possibility of a connection between the series of attacks you've suffered and the shootings here—"

"Not much gets past you boys, does it?"

"—MPD believes it important to extend our investigation. I have instructions to request a full local investigation, and to hand off responsibility for that investigation to your office. I'm doing so with this call."

"But suh, we don't know—"

"Shut up, Turner. Just be glad the FBI's not on its way down there."

He was right, of course.

"Turner…"

"Yeah?"

"I'm sorry for the way this went down. All of it."

"Thanks, Sam."

"We'll be expecting your reports, then. In due time. No particular hurry-up, we've got our hands full."

"Business as usual."

"God's truth. And Turner…"

"Yeah?"

"You do get up this way again, you should think about giving Tracy Caulding a call. For some twisted reason, the woman likes you."

"I know you find it hard to believe, Sam, but people do."

"Go figure... One hell of a world, ain't it?"

Chapter Twenty-Nine

It sure as hell is.

I didn't know exactly what it was that MPD expected us to investigate, but over the next several days I made gestures in that direction. J. T. had taken time off to head back up to Seattle—"thing or two I need to take care of." She'd left right before it happened, so I was pretty much running things.

I swung by Don Lee's that afternoon to see if he might be up to coming in to help. Patty Ann answered the door and told me how sorry she was. She said Don Lee was sleeping. The yeasty, rich smell of baking came from inside.

"He doing okay?" I asked.

"Just fine."

"Heard he'd been feeling bad."

She looked at me a moment before saying, "It comes

and goes. Kind of like Donald." She ducked her eyes, then added: "I can get him up for you."

"No, no. He needs his rest. Have him call me?"

"I'll do that. Time for a piece of pie before you go? I was just about to take it out of the oven."

"Best be going, but thanks."

Her gaze held mine. Something was pushing from inside, something that wanted to be said (about what had happened? about Don?) but never made it to the surface.

I stopped to help Sally Miller, whose car had stalled outside town, and pulled in at Lonnie's just behind Himself. He wore the usual khakis, which he must buy by the dozen, and a blue shirt. He had a sport coat tossed over one shoulder, his book bag over the other. The bag, he'd liberated from June years ago when she graduated high school, and now he took it everywhere. God knows what all's in there.

"Been on a jaunt, have we?"

"Little business I had to take care of, couldn't put it off any longer. How're you holding up?"

"I'm all right."

"Figuring I'd grab some late lunch and head down to the office, see what I could do to help."

Shirley opened the door as we stepped onto the porch. She gave me a hug, then hugged Lonnie. Inside she had a plate of sandwiches already made, fresh coffee in one of those pots that look like small urns.

"Call ahead and place an order?" I said.

He shrugged. Shirley smiled, said she was praying for us, and excused herself.

As he ate and I drank coffee, I told him about the call from Memphis.

"Full local investigation my ass," Lonnie said when I finished. Picking a divot of celery from between his teeth, he asked, "Those kids on the mountain doing okay?"

"Isaiah's back with them, cast and all. With everyone pitching in like they have, it's beginning to look good up there."

He got up, unplugged the pot and brought it over, poured more coffee for both of us.

"Is there anything you need, Turner? Anything I can do?"

"Just time…"

"Time, right. Worst enemy, best friend, all rolled into one. If there is anything—"

"I will, Lonnie."

"Like to think I don't need to say that."

"You don't."

"Good."

"This business of yours that came up…"

"Nothing much to it. Some old loose ends. It's done." He snagged another half sandwich, crusts cut off. This one was pimento cheese, which Shirley ground in an old hand-cranked processor heavy as an anvil. "We were worried about you, all alone up there at the cabin. Time like this, a man needs—"

"I was where I needed to be, Lonnie. Doing what I needed to do."

"Right. Who else would know, huh?"

"I'm fine."

Out in the living room, the TV was on and our current president, one of a cadre of archconservatives who had seized this country to wring its neck in the name of liberty, a man with a to-do list to whom everything was crystal clear, was speaking about "recent troubles in the old world." Yet again I marveled at how we always manage to persuade ourselves that our actions are justified, righteous, for the good.

"Thing is, you have to admire what those kids are doing up there," Lonnie said, "foolish as it is. They have an idea, a star to guide by, and they're willing to put everything they are behind it. How many of us can say that?"

J. T. got back to town not long after. I saw her pickup coming down the street, met her out front of the office. She looked exhausted—exhausted and wired—as she hauled a gym bag out of the cab and held it high to show this was the whole of it. Travel always does that, she said, stomps her flat, jacks her up. I filled her in on the call from Memphis. She listened carefully, shook her head and said nothing.

"So how'd it go?"

"Okay. How are you?"

"I've been worse. Get things taken care of?"

"Did my best, anyway."

"They still trying to get you back?"

"No. No, that's over. That's over, the flight's over, the drive's over—and I'm starved."

"Come on home with me, then. I'll cook."

She hesitated. "I don't think I want to be at the cabin just now, Dad."

"Fair enough, we'll go out. What are you up for?"

"Anything—as long as it's not the diner. No, I take that back. Meat. Serious meat."

And since Eldon was playing at the steakhouse an hour and spare change away, what better choice?

So we chose, and drove, only to find Eldon MIA. Said he had to be out of town a day or two, our waitress told us, her expression and inflection suggesting that she'd give damn near anything to be the same.

We'd made the drive with windows down, on deserted roads, through tide pools of moonlight and the smell of tomorrow's rain. It was at times like this, sitting together at the kitchen table or in a car, suspended for moments from causality and process, that the natural barriers between J. T. and myself receded. Not that they went down, just that they ceased for those suspended moments to matter.

"I've been thinking about my brother, about Don, a lot," she said. "Thinking how so many people I know have these lives that seem impossible to them. People who do really stupid things over and over. Stupid things, violent things—either to themselves or to others."

"Pain as the fulcrum, loss as the lever, to keep their worlds aloft. After a while that can get to be all they feel, all that reassures them they're alive."

"Exactly. You worked with them, Dad. You must understand."

"No. You always think you will. Every time you learn something new, develop a new passion, you think that's where you're heading. Like that song Eldon and Val used to sing. *Farther along we'll know all about it...* But you don't. You wind up holding the same blank cards—just more of them."

Despite Eldon's absence, we made the most of it, and of three or four pounds of steak between us, then drove back. It was not hard to imagine ghosts just off the road among the trees, riders out of a hundred Sleepy Hollows, fading echoes of great notions, fond hopes, and longed-for lives.

That night I heard, or dreamt I heard, a scratching at the screen on the window by my bed. I went out on the porch, but nothing was there. Only the old chair held together by twine, the stains on the floorboards. Nothing.

Chapter Thirty

Monday now. Before the call from Memphis, before my half-assed investigation. Or just *before*. Val and I are sitting on the porch.

"We're leaving in the morning, first light."

Instruments laid away in the back seat of the yellow Volvo, trailer hitched behind, road unfurling ahead. Westward ho.

Before.

"Like hunters."

"Exactly."

"I'll—"

"I know you will… I've already shut the house down. Thought I'd stay here tonight, if that's okay with you."

"Of course it is. Still planning on Texas as first stop?"

"As much as we're planning on anything. We'll get

in, point the car in that direction, see what happens."

I went in and got a bottle of wine I'd chilled the way she liked, rejoined her on the porch. I remember that the bottle had a colorful old-world label, red, yellow, purple, green, with a wooden gate or door on it; afterwards, when everyone was gone, I'd sit staring at it.

"You're okay as far as funds, right?"

"Jesus, you sound like a father sending his daughter off to school. But yeah, I'm good."

She picked up the glass, smelled the wine and smiled, put the glass down. Chill it, then let it sit to warm before drinking. There was this perfect moment in there somewhere.

"All these years, paycheck from the state, billings on clients, the only thing I ever spent money on's the house, and that was just for materials, since I—we— did the work. The rest I put away or, God help me, but I do drive a Volvo after all, invested. So I've got a raft that'll keep me afloat through the whitewater."

A ladybug lit on her glass, closing its wing case. Val watched as it traversed the rim.

"There's so much I'll miss," she said. "About the job, I mean—the rest goes without saying."

"Giving something back, making a difference, being a force for good…"

"Winning. Being right."

Neither of us said anything for a time. I sipped at my

wine. She anticipated hers.

"It scares me that so often that's what it comes down to. Which is as much as anything else why I need to stop. For now, anyway. Everything I've done, I start just trying to figure out how to get by. Not make a mess of it. Then before I know it, I've gotten serious about it, whatever it is—marble collecting, fencemending, it doesn't matter—and I'm trying to connect all the dots, trying to change things, make those marbles and fence slats *matter*. Turn those damn stupid marbles into whole round worlds."

She looked back at the ladybug, now on its third or fourth pass.

"The French call them *bêtes à bon dieu*," she said. "What a sweet, beautiful name."

"For so small and insignificant a thing."

"Exactly." She looked off to the trees. "The music will be the same. I know that."

Then: "The mythmakers had it wrong, Turner. It's not a clash of good and evil. It's a recondite war between the blueprinters, all those people who know just how things need to be and how to get that done, and the visionaries, who see something else entirely, and I've never been able to decide—"

"'Which side are you on, boys, which side are you on?'" Another old song.

"Right."

"We're all caught in the middle, Val."

"Which is why it's the stuff of myth."

Putting one leg up on the chair arm, she turned to me. The chair's joints went seriously knock-kneed, the twine that held them together at the point of letting go.

"There's a story I love, that I don't think I ever told you. Once, years ago, Itzhak Perlman was giving a concert at Carnegie Hall, some huge venue like that, and of course the house is packed. He hobbles onstage, puts aside his crutches, takes his seat. The orchestra begins, fades for his entrance, and when he hits the second or third note, a string breaks. Goes off like a shot. And everyone's figuring, Well, that's it. But very quietly Perlman signals the conductor to begin again—and he plays the entire concerto on three strings. You can all but see him rethinking the part in his head as he plays, rearranging it, recasting it, remaking it. And he does so faultlessly. 'You know,' he says afterwards, 'sometimes it is the artist's task to find out how much music you can still make with what you have left.'"

Smiling, she picked up her glass and lifted it to her mouth. I glanced away as the wings of a bird taking flight caught sunlight.

After the shot, I realized it had been quiet for some time. Night birds, frogs, none of them were calling. And I had missed it.

The sound of the glass shattering came close upon the shot. Val sat straight in the chair, her mouth opening twice as if to speak, then slumped. I went to her, expecting at any moment a second shot. As I held her, she pointed at the wine running slowly along the floorboards. The second shot came then—but from a shotgun, not a rifle.

Nathan stepped into the clearing, from lifelong habit extracting the shell casings and replacing them even as he moved forward. In moments he was there and had Val on the floor. We'd both seen our share of shootings, we knew what had to be done.

Later I'd learn that the kids up at the camp weren't the only ones Nathan had been keeping an eye on. He'd arrived after the man had taken his first shot and was preparing for the second. Must of heard the click of the safety release, Nathan said, 'cause he for damn sure didn't hear me, and looked round just in time to see both barrels coming at him.

No identification on the body, of course. Keys for a Camry that turned out not to be a rental but stolen, thick fold of hundreds and twenties in a money clip, full whiskey flask snugged in one rear pocket of his jeans. In the other they found a Congressional Medal of Honor.

J. T. came back to the cabin to tell me this.

"We might be able to trace him by it," she said,

"assuming of course that it's his."

But tracing him was dancing in place. We all knew that. We all knew where he came from. One dead soldier more or less, named or nameless, mattered little in the scheme of things.

"Dad?"

Only then did I realize I'd made no response.

"Are you going to be okay?"

Of course I would be, in time.

"You shouldn't be out here by yourself. Come on into town and stay with me, just for tonight."

But I declined, insisting that being by myself was exactly what I needed right now.

Again and again people say everything's a blur at these times, but it's not. For all that it happens fast, each single moment takes forever to uncoil in your mind, each image is clear and separate and rimed with light. Somewhere in my memory Val will always be sitting there slumped forward in the chair with a surprised expression on her face pointing to the spilled wine.

Lonnie showed up not long after, then Don Lee with Doc Oldham in tow. At one point Lonnie threatened to slap cuffs on me and haul my ass back to town if he had to. He didn't carry through on it, though. Most of us don't carry through; that's one of the things you can usually count on.

Eldon was the last to turn up, after the rest had gone,

even Nathan—though for all I knew, Nathan was still out there skulking. Eldon sat on the edge of the porch.

"I'm sorry, man," he said.

"We all are."

"You have no idea."

I didn't have much of anything.

"Rain heading this way."

"Good."

After a moment he said, "I loved her, John."

After a moment I said, "I know you did."

"What the hell are we gonna do now, man?"

"You're going to go on, to Texas and all those places you two had talked about, and you're going to play and sing the songs you and Val always did together."

I went in and got the banjo.

"She told me you were learning to play."

I don't think you can call what the banjo and I do together *play*. It's more of an adversary relationship."

When I handed it to him, he said, "I can't take this."

"Sure you can. It needs to be played, it needs to be allowed to do what it was made for."

We argued about it some more, and finally he agreed. "Okay, I'll take it, I'll even learn to play the thing. But it's not mine."

"That's what Val always said: that instruments don't belong to people, we just borrow them for a while."

"What about you? What are *you* going to do?"

I'm going to sit here on this porch, I told him. And once he was gone that's what I did, sat there on the porch looking out into the trees and back at the label on the wine bottle and thinking about the ragged edges of my life. About daybreak I saw Miss Emily walking at wood's edge with young ones in a line behind her. "Val," I said aloud, and as her name came back to me in echo from the trees it sounded very much like a prayer.

Somewhere deep inside myself I'm still sitting there, waiting.

ORDER THE COMPLETE JAMES SALLIS COLLECTION

Driven *(new title)*	978-184243-837-4	£7.99
The Long-Legged Fly	978-184243-696-7	£9.99
Moth	978-184243-700-1	£9.99
Black Hornet	978-184243-704-9	£9.99
Eye of the Cricket	978-184243-708-7	£9.99
Bluebottle	978-184243-712-4	£9.99
Ghost of a Flea	978-184243-716-2	£9.99
Cypress Grove	978-184243-728-5	£9.99
Cripple Creek	978-184243-732-2	£9.99
Salt River	978-184243-736-0	£9.99
Drive	978-184243-724-7	£9.99
The Killer is Dying	978-184243-740-7	£9.99
Death Will Have Your Eyes	978-184243-720-9	£9.99

Limited Edition Boxed Set   978-184243-886-2   £99
(Only 100 sets available containing all thirteen titles including *Driven*.
Plus a FREE twelve inch vinyl of James Sallis music and two short
stories specially recorded for this publication.)

Order online at www.noexit.co.uk/Sallis

Name:

Address:

Date: Order Number: Credit Card Number:

Expiry Date: Issue Number: Security Code (3 digit):

NO EXIT PRESS, PO Box 394, Harpenden, AL5 1XJ, U.K.
Tel: 01582 766348 or 020 7430 1021.
Free postage & packing in the UK, £10 for Euroland
and £20 for the Rest of the World.
For single copy orders £3.95 for Euroland
and £6.95 for the Rest of the World.
(Cheques in £Sterling drawn on UK bank payable to
Oldcastle Books Ltd)